"I need a mistress, a smokescreen."

Jake smiled. "Care to volunteer?"

"No, thanks," Stephanie said quickly.

"My dear Stephanie, would it be so terrible? I'd make it worth your while."

Anger sparked in her eyes. "How dare you!"

"You're prepared to do it *gratis*?" He was laughing now, showing fine white teeth. "For love?"

She had to get away, out of this room, away from his compelling presence. "I couldn't love you if you were the last man on earth," she spat. "And I won't act as your scapegoat, keeping your ex-wife at bay. Alana's your problem. You handle it—and her!"

But even as she spoke she knew it was a lie. With a little persuasion he could make her do anything. Anything at all....

D0017136

Books by Helen Bianchin

These books may be available at your local bookseller.

For a list of all titles currently available,
send your name and address to:

Harlequin Reader Service
P.O. Box 52040, Phoenix, AZ 85072-2040
Canadian address: P.O. Box 2800, Postal Station A,
5170 Yonge St., Willowdale, Ont. M2N 5T5

HELEN BIANCHIN

sweet tempest

Harlequin Books

TORONTO • NEW YORK • LONDON
AMSTERDAM • PARIS • SYDNEY • HAMBURG
STOCKHOLM • ATHENS • TOKYO • MILAN

Harlequin Presents first edition December 1984
ISBN 0-373-10744-7

Original hardcover edition published in 1984
by Mills & Boon Limited

CHAPTER ONE

BACCHUS MARSH in south-west Victoria was a pretty town, quiet for the most part, and close enough to Melbourne for its inhabitants to enjoy the pleasures of a large cosmopolitan metropolis with none of the disadvantages of city living.

Stephanie completed the last of her errands, then crossed the street to her car. It was cold, not quite sub-zero temperatures, but snow capped the distant mountains and the skies were heavy with impending rain.

Slipping in behind the wheel, she fired the engine, then eased the sleek blue Datsun 280ZX out into the stream of traffic. Huge droplets began to splatter the windscreen, and with a faint sigh she flicked on the wipers, adjusted the heating, then sent the car speeding west out of town.

The prospect of the weekend ahead was pleasing, despite her having no specific plans in mind. For the past three years she had acted as receptionist and general dogsbody for her father's veterinary practice, and although there were occasions when she missed the bustling Sydney hospital where she had completed her nursing training, she held no regrets about her present lifestyle.

Within minutes she reached the splendid stand of beech trees bordering their sprawling property and eased the car down the long gravelled driveway.

The house itself stood well back from the road,

a rambling double-storied grey stone structure with multi-paned windows picked out in white. An adjoining clinic, surrounded by ample parking space, lay to the right, and she garaged her car, then caught up her bag and made her way towards reception.

Slim and attractive, she looked much younger than her twenty-two years. Wavy ash-blonde hair tended to thicken into irrepressible curls unless checked, and its length cascaded on to her shoulders, providing a perfect foil for her delicately-moulded features. Possessing startling blue eyes that lightened or darkened with every mood change, she had a fascination that had been remarked upon by a veritable string of ardent males dating back to her first year in high school. By the time she joined the work-force her academic qualifications refuted a 'dizzy blonde' image, although the 'cute' label still remained, despite any effort to dispel it.

'Where have you been?'

Stephanie raised an enquiring eyebrow at the owner of that slightly harassed voice, and gave a deprecatory shrug as she slipped off her coat. 'I got delayed. Where's Dad?'

'In his office, waiting for you,' Michael responded dryly, his grimace deepening at her faintly puzzled expression. 'Of all the days to take an extended lunch break!'

In his late twenties, Michael had been her father's assistant for the past two years, and was someone with whom she shared an easy friendship.

'There was the banking, mail to collect, more to post,' she defended, wrinkling her nose at him. 'A few other things to attend to—all part of the job. Why?' she queried lightly. 'There are no appointments scheduled until three o'clock.'

'Patients—no,' he agreed, shooting her a wry glance. 'Your father, however, has been closeted with the owner of that impressive Lamborghini parked out front for almost an hour, and I've received no less than three directives to send you in the minute you arrive.'

'An exalted visitor?' she hazarded, mildly curious.

'God knows,' Michael dismissed. 'No ordinary mortal, for sure. It shows.'

'You're scaring me,' she joked, slanting him a grin. 'In that case, I'd better report for duty!' Placing her bag down on to the floor beside her desk, she walked to the door marked *Surgery*, tapped its panels lightly, then reached for the knob.

'Ah, there you are,' said Jim Matheson as she entered the room. There was no reproach in his voice, and she offered him a warm smile before letting her gaze drift casually to encompass the tall, dark-haired figure standing lazily at ease near the window.

In his mid-thirties and ruggedly male, he possessed an arresting, raw virility that would quicken the beat of many a feminine heart, she perceived wryly. A moustache graced his upper lip, shaped and wholly masculine, drawing attention to the sensual curve of his mouth, and his clothes bore a casual yet expensive elegance that sheathed his powerful frame as if they had been tailor-made.

'Jake, allow me to introduce my daughter. Stephanie—Jake Stanton.'

'Stephanie,' he acknowledged, his voice a deep drawl, and dark brown eyes pierced hers before embarking on a swift analytical appraisal.

All her fine body hairs rose in rapid instinctive

self-defence, and she managed a polite response before turning towards her father.

'You wanted to see me?'

His smile became gentle, his eyes warming with enthusiasm as he laced his fingers together on the desk-top. 'Remember the Veterinary Conference and series of lectures to be held in the States this month?' he prompted, and she searched the recesses of her mind for some vague recollection, yet found none. 'I didn't think I could get away,' he continued, not at all disturbed by her failure to recall such an important event. 'By a stroke of good fortune I happened to mention it to a retired colleague of mine. Bart rang last night to say his son had recently returned from Canada and would be willing to act as locum. After discussing details with Jake, I suggested he take the opportunity to familiarise himself with the clinic and meet the two people he'll be working with.'

The Conference obviously meant a great deal to him, and for his benefit Stephanie summoned as much enthusiasm as she could muster. 'How long will you be away?'

'Almost a month. Jake has excellent qualifications.' He gave a slight laugh, then added, 'With more than sufficient experience to run things in my absence.'

'When do you leave?'

'Monday.' He paused, then cleared his throat. 'Jake will naturally occupy one of the guest rooms in the house, and I've arranged for Edith James to stay over.'

That good lady had been their daily help for years, taking care of household chores and the preparation of their evening meals. A widow, she was well known for her kindheartedness, and

Stephanie breathed an inward sigh of relief. If first impressions amounted to anything, she'd need an adequate buffer against the cynical man destined to act as locum. Working with him would be bad enough—having him live in such close proximity was beginning to assume nightmarish proportion.

'Jake will arrive on Sunday,' her father continued as she endeavoured to mask her thoughts. 'Shall we say in time for lunch?'

'Of course,' Stephanie concurred evenly, her voice carefully polite.

'I'm quite used to simple fare,' Jake drawled, and gritting her teeth she summoned a slight smile.

'I'm an adequate cook, Mr Stanton.' God, if she didn't escape soon, she'd say something reprehensible! 'If you'll excuse me? I'd better get back to reception.' She studiously swung her attention towards her father. 'Unless I'm mistaken, that's Mrs Woods' Bartholomew registering disapproval at being kept waiting!' Her exit was smoothly effected, but not before she caught the wry cynicism evident in Jake Stanton's expression.

Damn, damn, *damn*, she cursed inconsequentially. Four whole weeks in that sardonic man's company. How on earth was she going to survive?

There were three reluctant canine patients in the company of their owners awaiting attention, and Stephanie dealt with each of them in turn, extracting files and marking the appointment book accordingly before despatching a sweet-natured Labrador and her equally sweet owner into Michael for a routine injection. Bartholomew was something else, and she had little hesitation in alerting her father via the intercom that the highly-strung dog was fast becoming neurotic.

She was aware of the moment Jake Stanton

took his leave, and it didn't help that she was in a position where a dignified, even aloof, farewell was impossible. Perched high on the third step of a ladder in the midst of collecting a file for an incoming patient, and with no less than four people with four pets of varying description as interested bystanders, she could only afford him a polite farewell before going about her business as if his presence had had no effect on her at all.

When the last patient for the day had been attended to, Stephanie put the cover over her typewriter, locked the outer door, then slipped into the surgery.

'So—we're to have a new boss as from Monday,' Michael declared, shooting her one of his wolfish grins.

'Only for a month,' she returned swiftly, and glimpsed his silent laughter.

'*Wow!*' he derided softly. 'And our new locum gets to stay in the house, too. What will the boyfriend have to say about that, I wonder?'

'Friend,' she corrected. 'Anyway, what can Ian object to? Mrs James will be there.'

'Did you get a look at him? Sweet mother in heaven, girl—he's dynamite!'

'He is?' she arched deliberately. 'Funny, he doesn't grab me at all.'

'Not yet, but what's the betting he will before the month is out?'

'He won't stand a chance with Satan sleeping outside my bedroom door, and Mrs James occupying the room next to mine.' She shot him a cross look. 'Besides, there's Ian to consider.'

He simulated a mocking leer. 'My dear, you could do so much better with almost anyone else. Even me. I like you an awful lot—I even respect and admire you. Certainly, I could love you without any effort at all. Yet you consistently refuse every invitation I extend. Why? is what I want to know. Is it something my best friends won't tell me about?'

Stephanie picked up a near-by pencil and threw it at him. 'Wretch! You know perfectly well I like you.'

His expressive features assumed wry humour. 'Sure—as a brother.'

'Do me a favour,' she began slowly, letting her lashes veil her eyes.

'Anything. Ask, and it shall be done.'

'Fool! Seriously,' she admonished.

'Okay—*seriously*.'

'Keep Jake Stanton off my back. He—irritates me.'

'That's tantamount to an admission of sorts,' Michael pronounced wickedly. 'Perhaps I should move in temporarily and keep an eye on the both of you.'

'One day,' she threatened mockingly, shaking her fist at him, 'I'm going to do you an injury!'

'Promises, promises,' he grinned, unabashed, and she gave a prodigious sigh.

'I'm off to the house. Dad will be back from the Edwards' farm in an hour. That will give me time to shower, finish off whatever preparations Mrs James has made for dinner, then afterwards I'm going to retire early to bed with a book.'

'What a waste—when you could be out on the town with me.'

'You're all talk, Michael,' she grinned. 'If perchance I took you up on any one of your many invitations, you'd backtrack so fast you'd fall over your own feet!'

'Try me!'

'Maybe I will—next week.'

'Name a night.'

She leant out a hand and gave him a friendly push. 'Oh, go home. I have more important things to do than stand here exchanging nonsensical banter with you!'

'I'm deeply hurt.'

Stephanie pulled a face at him, then turned and left the clinic by the side door. The outside air was fresh and cool, and she hurried towards the house, let herself into the kitchen, then crossed to the table to read the note Edith James had left propped up against the sugar bowl. A casserole reposed in the oven, vegetables were ready in their saucepans atop the stove, and there was an apple pie cooling in the pantry.

Over dinner Jim Matheson was elated about his proposed trip, and Stephanie endeavoured to be enthusiastic for his benefit. If the truth be known, getting away would do him the world of good, for he hadn't had a break during the past three years. Together they sifted through numerous brochures, traced the various routes and stopovers, then by mutual consent viewed a television documentary until it was time to go to bed.

The following day became a flurry of activity, with morning surgery proving even more demanding than usual, and no less than four emergency calls during the afternoon and early evening.

Consequently when Ian called shortly after seven, Stephanie viewed their impending date with something less than enthusiasm. Of all things, it was a party, and any attempt to get him to leave early was thwarted by the obviously great time he was having. Rather wearily she bore with him until

shortly after midnight, then sensing her obvious reluctance to stay longer, he allowed her to lead him
out to the car. Her quiet insistence on taking the
wheel was met with a philosophical shrug, and when
she deposited him outside his home his clumsy attempt to kiss her was something less than desirable.
All in all, it was a forgettable evening, and later in bed
on the edge of sleep Jake Stanton's forceful image
rose to taunt her. She saw his enigmatic, faintly sardonic smile, the cynical gleam in the depths of his
eyes, and not for the first time she cursed the circumstances that were about to throw them together.

Sunday dawned with dismal showers and the
promise of more to come. Stephanie spent the
hours before breakfast alternating whether to
prepare an elaborate luncheon, or stick with
something simple, like soup followed by steak and
an assortment of vegetables, with stewed fruit and
fresh cream to follow. In the end, she elected to
roast a leg of pork with all the accompaniments,
then serve a light evening meal.

Around eleven o'clock she began to get tense
and edgy, one ear straining for the sound of a car
pulling to a halt in the driveway. It was crazy to
feel this way over a relative stranger. He had
shown no particular interest in her at all, and there
was no reason to suppose the ensuing four weeks
shouldn't go smoothly. Her father appeared
impressed with Jake Stanton's ability, and had no
qualms that he wouldn't be able to cope. As to the
qualities of the man himself, it was doubtful he
had even given them a thought. Jake's being the
son of a friend and fellow colleague undoubtedly
exonerated any misgivings.

The temptation to invite Ian for lunch was
great, but at the last moment she decided it might

not be such a good idea. Her father would want to discuss the clinic, bring various aspects of it to his locum's attention, and Ian was not a lover of animals. It wasn't that he disliked them, simply admitted they held no appeal.

Stephanie decided to serve lunch at one, and at twelve-thirty she crossed to the dining room and set the table, following her mother's tradition in utilising one of the fine damask cloths, the silver cutlery, and crystal goblets. It was something she liked to continue, for her father's sake, like ensuring that there were always fresh flowers in the lounge and the study, a supply of his favourite raspberry jam. After her mother's death, he had expressed the desire that everything should proceed exactly as before, and with Edith James' collaboration she saw that it did.

At ten to one Stephanie put the plates to warm in the oven, removed her apron, then went upstairs to change. Deliberately understating her appearance, she selected a woollen skirt and topped it with a lambswool jumper of soft lilac. Make-up comprised a light dusting of powder and a touch of lipstick. Casting her hair a wry glance, she took up her brush and attempted to restore a measure of order to the mass of riotous curls, then she hurried quickly downstairs in search of her father. If Jake Stanton hadn't arrived, she could delay lunch by as much as half an hour. Beyond that, it would spoil.

She found him in the study, engrossed in conversation with their guest, and she endeavoured not to show her surprise. It was feasible that any sound of the man's arrival had been masked by the very recent fall of rain, but it was irritating to think he'd been here in the house without her knowledge.

'Ah, come in, my dear,' Jim Matheson beamed, his gesture expansive, and there was little else she could do but cross to his side.

With considerable civility she let her gaze swing towards the man standing close by, and her smile was polite. 'I see you've arrived, Mr Stanton.'

'An hour ago,' he informed her imperturbably, his slanting glance faintly cynical as it rested on her slightly flushed cheeks. 'Perhaps you won't find it too difficult to use my christian name?' he added sardonically, and Jim Matheson glanced from one to the other, then let his eyes rest on his daughter's fair head.

'Have you come to fetch us in to lunch, darling?'

'Whenever you're ready,' Stephanie told him, deliberately widening her smile. 'Five minutes, okay?'

'We'll be there,' he promised, his expression becoming faintly pensive as he watched her departure.

Lunch was not the easiest of meals—at least, not as far as Stephanie was concerned. She was made increasingly aware of the man seated at her left, her senses heightened by some elusory magnetic pull that angered as much as it intrigued.

On the surface, Jake Stanton was friendly, including her in the conversation whenever he deigned it necessary to acknowledge her presence. Yet there was an aloofness, almost a detached uninterest barely evident, that rankled slightly. Not, she assured herself, that she wanted him to bestow her any attention. His appearance gave every indication that he was more than any one woman could handle—at least, any woman with a grain of common sense!

Fortunately her father refrained from giving

overt praise with regard to her culinary expertise, although her efforts didn't go unnoticed and she earned an acknowledgment, pleasantly given, from their guest, and only she was aware of the faint mockery evident.

It was a relief when the two men excused themselves from the table and left the room. With a bit of luck they would disappear into the clinic and wouldn't be seen again until it was time for dinner!

After loading the dishwasher and dispensing with numerous pots and pans Stephanie escaped upstairs and entered her father's room with the intention of selecting sufficient of his clothes as she thought necessary, then, the chore completed, she laid them out on the bed, leaving him the final choice.

The room Jake Stanton had been assigned was immediately opposite, and she gave a faint grimace as she passed the closed door. Why did she suddenly have the feeling that his presence had already wrought a subtle change in the happy carefree atmosphere that had always been evident in her home? The instinctive knowledge that things would never be the same again prompted her to snatch up a sheepskin-lined jacket from her bedroom at the far end of the hall, then almost running downstairs she collected her car keys and headed for the garage.

Oddly restless, she reversed out and headed down the drive, turning in the direction of town. There were any number of friends she could visit, and without any forethought she found herself turning into the street where Ian lived with his mother.

Her arrival was scheduled, and she felt vaguely

irritated by the fact that impromptu visits were considered an infringement of Mrs Bryant's privacy.

At least Ian's response didn't lack enthusiasm, and she accepted his kiss with more warmth than usual.

A pleasant young man, fair-haired and of medium height, he was someone she'd grown up with, and over the past year their friendship had developed into an affectionate bond.

'Stephanie! Lovely to see you.' He gave her a hug and placed his arm about her shoulders, leading her indoors. 'I thought you'd be too busy this afternoon.'

How could she explain the need to get out of her own home, away from the disturbing man, who, even on so short an acquaintance, gave sensual perception a depth of meaning she was loath to explore. Or to add that she had obeyed a primeval instinct to run as fast and as far as her legs would carry her!

'Mother and I were just about to have afternoon tea,' Ian elaborated, pushing open the lounge door. 'You must join us.'

Why did the thought of an apparently rugged young man spending his time partaking of such a traditional repast rankle? Most men of a similar age were out playing football, rugby, golf—or an equally strenuous indoor sport. Not, she decided reluctantly, that Ian's devotion to his widowed mother wasn't commendable. Except that Mrs Bryant regarded anyone, male or female, as a threat to the hold she retained on her son.

'Look who's called in to see us,' Ian announced with a wide grin, and he missed the sudden tightening of the older woman's lips, the faint bleakness that made her pale blue eyes seem even paler.

'Stephanie.' Her acknowledgment was perfunctory, and stiltedly polite. 'Do come in and sit down.'

An hour was more than Stephanie could conceivably bear, and afterwards she wondered why she hadn't simply stayed at home and contacted Ian by phone. It would have been infinitely preferable to the tête-à-tête she'd had to endure!

She arrived home just as the grandfather clock in the hall struck four, and retrieved the note propped up against the vase of flowers on the dining-room table. A hollow laugh bubbled up inside her throat. Her escape had been in vain. Her father had been called out unexpectedly and had taken Jake Stanton with him. Unless there were any unforeseen complications, they would be back in time for dinner.

Stephanie crumpled the note and aimed it for the waste basket in the kitchen. It was idiotic to succumb to such a contrary mood. Normally sunny-natured and serene as she was, this sudden illogical mood-swing was something she found difficult to assimilate, and in a determined effort to dispel it she went into the kitchen, withdrew a recipe book from among its companions, then spent time deliberating what form dessert would take for the evening meal.

By the time the two men returned two hours later she had her wayward emotions under control, and she faced Jake Stanton across the dining-room table with admirable panache, utilising all her capabilities in the role of hostess to lead her father into revealing various amusing anecdotes relating to the clinic and its patients, so that before the men were aware of it, they had finished the delectable dessert and were being encouraged to retreat into the study for coffee.

Thereafter it was relatively simple to pretend the need for an early night in view of her father's early departure next morning.

Ensconced in bed with a book, she gave her watch a derisory glance and conceded that the last time she'd retired this early was while she was still at school and cramming for an exam!

She read for an hour, then switched off the light in an attempt to covet sleep. Except that enviable escape into blissful oblivion proved elusive, and she lay awake long into the early morning hours, slipping into an uneasy somnolence that became fraught with dark dreams, so that she woke pale and heavy-eyed shortly after the new day's dawn.

CHAPTER TWO

'BYE, darling. Take care of yourself,' Jim Matheson bade his daughter as his flight was called over the tannoy. 'I'll ring you from the hotel in Los Angeles.' His kindly face creased with momentary concern. 'Don't worry, Stephanie. Jake is well able to cope, and Edith James will be there by the time you get home.'

Heavens, she'd have to perk up a bit, otherwise he would develop second thoughts about going, and that wouldn't be fair. He deserved the break, his first in too many years.

'Worry?' she arched with a grin, giving him a quick hug. 'Who's worrying? Everything will go so smoothly, I doubt your absence from the clinic will even be noticed,' she added teasingly, relieved as a smile widened his lips. 'Now, go through the barrier,' she ordered, giving him a gentle push. 'That was the last call.' She stood on tiptoe and kissed his weatherbeaten cheek, summoned a lopsided smile as he leant out a hand and ruffled the mass of curls framing her face, and she managed a cheery wave as he turned for the last salute before disappearing out of sight.

Tullamarine International Airport was a hive of activity, and Stephanie moved with the crowd towards the observation deck, electing to wait until the giant Boeing 747 soared into the sky. Perhaps it was sentimentality, but she preferred to actually see her father safely airborne.

It was almost eleven o'clock when she turned

the Datsun into the driveway and brought it to a smooth halt inside the garage. There were several cars lining the parking space adjacent the clinic, and her lips formed a faint grimace. It hadn't taken long for news of a new locum to spread round the district.

The waiting room was almost full, and she crossed to her desk and slid into her chair.

'Jim get away okay?' asked Michael, slanting a quizzical eyebrow in silent acknowledgment of their influx of patients.

'Yes, no problems or delays,' she said quietly, running her eye over the array of files lying neatly beside the typewriter. 'Any messages?'

'Several, but only one personal one. Amy Collins has rung three times—wants you to contact her urgently.'

A slight frown creased her forehead. 'Amy?' Recognition returned as she recalled Edith James had a daughter of that name. 'Oh, *Amy*. Sure, I'll make the call now.' Her fingers were already lifting the receiver, and she dialled the required digits with professional speed.

'Thank heavens!' a sensible feminine voice greeted on the third ring. 'I'm afraid I have bad news. Mum slipped down the stairs this morning and broke her leg.'

'Oh, that's too bad,' Stephanie responded immediately. 'I hope it's only a simple fracture. Is there anything I can do?'

'Not a thing,' the other woman returned at once. 'Although Mum is dreadfully upset at having to leave you in the lurch.'

Stephanie's stomach muscles tightened fractionally as the implication of Edith James' absence began to sink in. Her fingers clutched the receiver and she endeavoured to keep her voice light. 'She mustn't worry about it, Amy. We'll be able to manage—and anyway,' she added, her mind spinning rapidly ahead, 'I'm sure I can find a replacement, and even if I can't, it won't be the end of the world.' The light on the small switchboard began to glow, signifying that there was another call waiting. 'Can you hold, Amy? Or shall I ring back?'

'I'm on my way to the hospital. I'll check with you later in the day.'

Stephanie depressed a switch, then flicked up another, taking the incoming call with professional courtesy. It transpired that a distraught owner needed urgent reassurance and she transferred the call to Surgery.

'Yes?' Jake Stanton's voice sounded curt and unfamiliar, and for some reason a tiny shiver feathered its way down her spine.

'Mrs Johnson's Tabitha has eaten three of her sutures, and nothing will stop her attacking those remaining,' she reported briskly. 'Will you speak to her?'

'Tabitha?'

His cynical drawl made her catch her breath, and it was all she could do not to snap back at him.

'Not unless you possess some mystical powers in feline communication,' she answered dryly, and put through the call without waiting for him to comment.

Mondays were usually busy, and today was no exception. So much so that it was another hour before Stephanie had an opportunity to put a call through to the town's principal employment agency to request a replacement for Edith James.

The receptionist promised to do her best, but finding someone who was prepared to live in would be difficult.

'You look vaguely harassed. What's up?'

She glanced up and caught Michael's intent stare. 'You wouldn't believe me if I told you,' she revealed with slight disparagement. 'Do me a favour and switch lunches? I have to organise something edible for our inestimable locum.'

One eyebrow rose quizzically. 'Don't you trust the capable Mrs James to feed him?'

'I would, if she could,' Stephanie grimaced. 'However, she'd find that a bit difficult from a hospital bed.'

A soft whistle left his lips. 'You're not serious?'

'Oh, infinitely,' she sighed wearily. 'Now, will you switch?'

'Sure. Anything to please.'

'Your solicitude is commendable,' a sardonic voice intruded. 'If I might suggest you confine your working hours to *work*?'

Stephanie closed her eyes momentarily in an effort to restrain her temper. He really was the limit! With admirable calm she rose to her feet and proferred Michael a singularly sweet smile. 'I'll be back in an hour.'

'Going somewhere?' Jake queried idly, and she turned to face him—a mistake, for she was immediately at a disadvantage.

Slowly she let her eyes travel up the strong column of his throat, glimpsed the firm chin, the wide sensuously moulded mouth, then reluctantly met his enigmatic gaze. He had to know some time, and it might as well be now. 'Mrs James is in hospital,' she said evenly. 'I'm taking an early lunch-break in order to fix you something to eat.'

His regard was startlingly level. 'Presumably you've endeavoured to find a replacement?'

'I have—so far without any success,' she told him tartly. 'I'll make a few more calls from the house.'

Jake's gaze narrowed, and his expression became an enigmatic mask. 'I have some business to attend to in town. I'll get something there.'

She effected a slight shrug. 'As long as it's no inconvenience.'

'None at all,' he said dryly, moving aside.

Stephanie stepped past him, hating the way her pulse quickened in awareness of his close proximity. It wasn't until she was out of the clinic and walking towards the house that she began to breathe evenly. Damn him! she cursed ineffectually as she entered the side door and moved into the kitchen. She didn't know him at all, yet already she hated him. He had the oddest effect on her equilibrium, making her aware of latent sensations that were both unenviable and unwanted. It hadn't been so bad, knowing that there would be someone else in the house to act as a buffer, but now the prospect of four long weeks seemed to stretch interminably.

The likelihood of engaging household help at such short notice didn't augur well, and after consulting three agencies she was inclined to agree that while it was possible to engage a daily woman, finding someone unencumbered by family responsibilities which would enable them to live in looked like proving a hopeless task.

Meantime, there was dinner to think about, and with this in mind Stephanie crossed to the refrigerator and extracted some steak from the well-stocked deepfreeze. While there she removed some beef with which to prepare a casserole for tomorrow's lunch. Somehow she imagined Jake Stanton possessed a hearty appetite—he'd certainly done justice to the three meals she had prepared so far.

Aware that her lunch hour was almost over, she caught up a piece of bread, buttered and folded it over a piece of ham, then poured a glass of fruit juice. Not much in the way of sustenance, she grimaced wryly as she finished both, and supplemented it with a banana, tucking the fruit into her pocket, assuring herself she'd eat it during the afternoon.

There was little time to do anything other than work during the ensuing five hours. The phone rang constantly, filling the appointment book over the following few days to such an extent that Stephanie began to wonder how many cases were actually genuine.

As was customary, she managed to slip away from the clinic shortly after five-thirty, and knowing there had been no emergency calls to delay dinner, she set about preparing vegetables for the evening meal.

She heard Jake enter the house just as she was about to heat some soup from the vast quantity Edith James had prepared a few days previously, and immediately the muscles in her stomach tensed into a painful knot.

Fool, she told herself silently. He's everything you dislike in a man, so why react like a teenage schoolgirl?

'Any luck in acquiring a housekeeper?'

Stephanie put down the bowl, then placed a lid on top of the saucepan. 'None,' she responded civilly. 'All three agencies assure me it will be almost impossible to engage someone to live in at such short notice. However, there's hope a daily woman can be found before the end of the week.' She spared him a glance, then wished she hadn't. His tall frame was intimidating, and there was only austere remoteness in his expression. 'Until then, I can manage,' she continued stiltedly.

'I'm sure you can,' Jake commented dryly.

Oh Lord, he didn't plan on making the situation any easier! A smile, or at least commiseration at their fate, would have a lightening effect. As it was, he was being a positive bear!

Aloud, she declared, 'Dinner will be ready in twenty minutes, if you want to shower or shave. There's beer in the fridge, and an assortment of spirits in the lounge cabinet. I'm sure Dad has told you to help yourself.'

'Is that a polite way of banishing me from the kitchen?'

She closed her eyes momentarily in an effort to remain calm. 'Why would you want to stay?' she asked simply, and saw his lips twist to form a wry smile.

'Twenty minutes?'

'Yes.'

Then he was gone, and she let out an inaudible sigh of relief. This was only the beginning. There were four weeks to get through, and even culling a wild social existence wouldn't dispose of the inevitable hours they would come in contact with each other.

After setting the table and checking the contents in various saucepans, she removed the apron she had tied about her waist on entering the kitchen, then cast her watch a hurried glance. She had ten minutes in which to shower and change, and she moved across the hall, taking the stairs with graceful agility.

The house was old, built of well-preserved stone and timber with large high-ceilinged rooms and wide passageways. Although it was comfortable, its design precluded modern en suite facilities, and the upstairs bedrooms were served by two bathrooms, one at each end of the hall.

Just as she reached the top of the stairs a door opened to her left and Jake emerged from the bathroom, a towel hitched about his waist and another slung carelessly over one shoulder.

Quickly averting her eyes, she moved towards her own room with more haste than usual, then cursed herself for being so naïve. She had seen the male form adorned in far less on numerous occasions during her nursing years, and there was no reason for an expanse of tanned muscled flesh to create so much havoc within her feminine breast!

Thoroughly cross, she caught up a change of clothes from her room, then went into her bathroom and showered with admirable speed. Dressed, she smoothed moisturiser over her face, and declined any further use of make-up. Damned if she would give him any reason to suppose she might find him attractive by taking undue care with her appearance!

In the kitchen she deftly set about serving the food on to plates, then placed them into the oven to keep warm while they had the soup. Fresh fruit salad and cream would have to suffice as dessert.

Jake was in the lounge, and he turned as she entered the room. He held a glass in his hand, and dark trousers topped with a casual vee-necked jumper served to accentuate his male physique.

'It's ready?' His query was a light mocking drawl, and she stiffened imperceptibly.

'Yes.'

He drained the remains of his glass in a single long swallow, and Stephanie mentally shuddered, imagining the unpalatableness of raw spirit coursing down his throat.

His smile became vaguely cynical. 'Have I suddenly grown horns?'

She met his dark gaze and held it, then offered politely, 'The soup will be getting cold.'

His head inclined in a mocking slant. 'Ah, the soup. By all means let's observe the conventions.' His arm swept out in an arc as he stood to one side. 'After you.'

Stephanie was aware of him walking behind her, and to her chagrin she felt all her nerve-ends tingle damnably alive.

The dining-room table was oval in shape, and she had deliberately set a place at each end. The soup tureen reposed in the middle, and she reached for the ladle.

'For God's sake, sit down,' Jake instructed brusquely. 'I'm not exactly a guest. I can easily serve myself.'

She drew in a deep breath, then expelled it slowly. 'I'm merely extending you the same courtesy I would my father.'

He took the ladle from her nerveless fingers, then leaned forward and picked up her plate. When both plates had been filled he ventured matter-of-factly, 'I take it you switched the phone over from the clinic?'

Almost on cue, it rang. 'Does that answer your query?' Stephanie asked, getting to her feet to answer it.

'Is that you, Stephanie?' Ian queried, and she felt inclined to snap that it was hardly likely to be anyone else.

'We're in the middle of dinner,' she said smoothly. 'Can I ring you back?'

'Actually, I thought you might like to ask me over.'

With no need to ask the reason why, she decided ruefully. 'Not tonight, Ian. I have rather a lot to do.'

'Just for an hour or so,' he inveigled. 'Please!'

She released an expressive sigh. 'I'm sorry. Maybe tomorrow?'

His response was eager. 'Invite me for dinner?'

Oh, *hell*, she groaned inwardly. Having to field a conversational gambit with Jake Stanton was bad enough—Ian's presence would only serve to heighten a difficult situation. Yet Ian was a regular weekly visitor at their dinner table, and she could hardly hurt his feelings by suddenly refusing to invite him. Aloud she said brightly, 'Sure, why not? Around six? Now I must go.'

'Boy-friend?'

Stephanie shot the owner of that soft mocking drawl a defensive glance and decided a little subterfuge wouldn't do any harm. 'Yes,' she acknowledged briefly, picking up her spoon. 'He's coming to dinner tomorrow night.'

'Is that a subtle hint for me to absent myself from the house?'

Her eyes flew wide, and their depths held sparks of anger. 'Of course not. I've known Ian practically all my life.'

'I see.'

Incensed, she demanded, 'What do you see, Mr Stanton?'

'Jake,' he insisted quietly, and she inclined her head with exaggerated mockery.

'All right—*Jake*.'

One eyebrow lifted as he regarded her silently, then he queried with a silkiness that smothered any further retort, 'Shall I get the next course?'

Sheer bravado was responsible for her holding his gaze for a further heartstopping few seconds, then she conceded defeat by returning her attention to her partly filled plate. 'It's in the oven.'

Jake stood to his feet with an easy litheness that denoted physical fitness and moved towards the kitchen, returning within minutes with both plates, placed hers within reach and then resumed his seat at the opposite end of the table.

Stephanie finished her soup and looked at the succulent steak and accompanying vegetables with something akin to distaste. If she ate it, the food would surely stick in her throat.

'Are you going to eat it, or simply look at it?' Jake queried dryly, and she glanced up to see that he was waiting for her to start.

'Do go ahead,' she said quickly. 'Besides, I'm not hungry.'

He shot her a dark level glance, then returned his attention to the food on his plate. 'I'd like to go over tomorrow's appointments and check out the respective files. I imagine your filing system is straightforward?'

She prided herself on its simplistic accessibility, and resented his sardonic inference that it might be one only she could understand. 'Up until now no one has had any problems with it.' She directed him a tight smile, offering sweetly, 'However, there's always a first time.'

His lips curved into a wry smile. 'Point taken.'

It was a relief when the meal was over, and Jake's departure from the house soon afterwards made it easy for her to restore the kitchen to its pristine state. There were countless chores to catch up on, and she set about them with contrived enthusiasm. A phone call to the hospital elicited the news that Edith James was as comfortable as could be expected, and a message was left to the effect that Stephanie would visit the following evening.

At nine-thirty she connected the electric kettle and made herself some coffee. Satan, the black and tan German Shepherd, whined at the french doors, and she rose to let him in. His soulful eyes cast a sweeping search of the room, then he slumped down at her feet in mute despair.

'I know,' she consoled, bending down to scratch behind his ears. 'We're all alone, aren't we?'

Her eyelids began to droop, and she forced them wide in an effort to stay awake, then became cross with herself. Why should she stay up, for heaven's sake? Standing to her feet, she crossed to the phone and lifted the receiver.

It rang twice, then Jake answered. 'An emergency call?'

'No,' she said shortly. 'I'm going to bed. There's some coffee on the stove, and I've left some biscuits, if you want them.' She hardly paused, giving him no time to comment. 'Everything is locked except the side door. Goodnight.'

The insistent peal of the alarm penetrated Stephanie's subconscious, and with a groan she rolled over and reached out a hand to switch it off. Six o'clock. It was still dark, but as she swept open

the drapes the sky was tinged with the first
opalescent tinge of dawn, and even as she watched
the horizon began to lighten, bathing everything
beneath it with a shadowy glow. There was a
curious stillness in the air, a sort of waiting
expectancy for the birth of a new day. Trees
glistened, their leaves dew-kissed, and she spied a
large spider's web in the garden below, crystallised
in symmetrical splendour against a backdrop of
dark foliage. A light breeze stirred softly along the
ground, lifting the fallen autumn leaves and
swirling them into strange eddying patterns.

A faint whicker from the direction of the stables
indicated that Clara, the elderly mare, was on her
feet and ready for an early morning trot round the
paddock.

Scrambling into jeans and a thick woollen
jumper, Stephanie made quickly for the bathroom,
sluiced water over her face and cleaned her teeth,
then dragged a brush through her hair before
running lightly downstairs.

It was more than an hour before she re-entered
the house, having fed and exercised Clara, fed the
three dogs, four cats, checked the aviary, moved
Siegfried the goat to a fresh clump of long grass,
and mixed the mash for the assortment of poultry
and collected their eggs. As was his usual custom,
Satan had ambled at her heels, showing patience
as he skirted the recalcitrant rooster who provided
her with a battle of wills on every occasion she
stepped into his territory. Now she took food from
the refrigerator and set it on Satan's plate, then
did likewise for Sasha the house cat.

It was after seven, and she'd just have time for a
quick shower before making breakfast. Of Jake
there was no sign, and she stifled a wry grimace.

Somehow he didn't appear the type to oversleep, and even as she dismissed the thought his bedroom door opened and he stepped out into the hallway.

'Good morning.' His greeting was polite, his smile little more than a slight twist of his lips. Levi's hugged his lean hips, and a workmanlike sweater in fine black wool stretched itself over broad shoulders, accentuating a goodly share of muscle and sinew.

Her acknowledging nod was tempered with a faint frown. 'I'll be down to make breakfast in about ten minutes. Have you any preference? Or is steak and eggs okay?'

'I'll fix it myself,' said Jake, and her eyes were remarkably clear as she met his gaze.

'There's no need.' She gave a light shrug. 'I always cook Dad's breakfast. Why should cooking yours make any difference?'

His eyes ran sharply over her appearance, his gaze swift and all-encompassing. 'Do I have to repeat myself? I'm not a guest, and don't intend being treated as one. From the look of you, you've already attended to the animals. I'll take a turn tomorrow,' he finished curtly.

'Why?' she demanded simply. 'I always do it.'

'Do you enjoy being a martyr?' he queried cynically, and she returned hotly,

'You've been employed as my father's locum— not a general helping hand!'

'Tell me,' Jake drawled, 'are you always so damned argumentative?'

She took a deep breath and endeavoured not to lose her temper. 'The clinic opens in just over an hour. I haven't got *time* to argue.' Her eyes became deep blue chips and her lips tightened. 'Make your own breakfast if it's that darned important!'

His mouth slanted into a sloping smile. 'Is the boy-friend aware you're something of a shrew this early in the morning?'

'He doesn't rile me the way you do!' Stephanie flung incautiously, and without a further word she brushed past him and swept into her room.

It was a hollow victory, and when she thought about it, no victory at all. With angry actions she discarded her clothes and slipped beneath the shower to emerge minutes later, then towelled dry, she slipped quickly into fresh underwear, pulled on her dressing-gown and returned to her room.

There she donned a warm skirt and jumper over which she slipped a pale blue shortsleeved nylon uniform. She left the buttons undone, then quickly made her bed, straightened the covers and crossed to the mirrored dressing-table where she applied moisturiser, a touch of eyeshadow, and ran the brush through her hair.

Downstairs she crossed towards the kitchen and breathed in the mouthwatering aroma of freshly-brewed coffee. Satan was lolling on the floor, his head between his paws, and he looked up soulfully as she swung open the door.

'Yours is in the warming drawer of the oven,' Jake declared from the table. 'There's plenty of toast, and at least two cups of coffee left in the pot.'

'I usually have fruit and cereal.'

'And it would be impossible to vary it, I suppose,' he queried dryly.

'Not at all.' Her smile was very sweet, although her eyes held no hint of humour.

'Do you have any objection if I skim through the paper?'

'By all means,' she agreed magnanimously, glad

of the opportunity to eat without being aware of his watchful scrutiny, and crossing to the oven she extracted the plate and placed it on the table.

After five minutes, Jake drained the last of his coffee and stood to his feet. 'I'll go and open up the clinic.'

Stephanie didn't bother to comment, and barely resisted the temptation to poke out her tongue at his departing back. Alone, she picked up another piece of toast, buttered it and spread it with jam, then poured herself a second coffee. A sudden thought came to mind and she muffled an unladylike curse. Lunch—she had a casserole to put in the oven. And Ian was coming for dinner.

It was almost eight-thirty when she walked through the clinic door, and Michael glanced up from speaking on the phone and pointed silently to his watch.

Slipping behind the desk, she pulled forward the appointment book and noted that the morning's allocation of files were already arranged in order. A faint grimace creased her features. Jake, no doubt, was responsible. Instead of being grateful, she felt annoyed and elected to think he hadn't bothered to return them after his perusal the previous evening.

There was a brisk number of calls throughout the morning, of which two were from employment agencies. One told her they could supply a daily help as from the following week, the other was slightly better in that they had a woman on their books who was prepared to start the next day. As to her request for someone to live in, both declared they had conducted a thorough check of their files and made numerous enquiries, without success. Rather wearily Stephanie instructed the second agency to send someone the following day. At least it would ease the situation considerably having household chores and meals taken care of, she decided philosophically.

Jake was called out just before lunch and she extracted sufficient for herself, then returned the casserole to the oven. Caught up in a flurry of activity during her customary break, she decided she had to be mad letting Ian come tonight. There was hardly any time to prepare a satisfactory meal, and she still hadn't rung the hospital to enquire about Edith James. A frown creased her forehead, then disappeared. Ian could drive her up there tonight. It would give her an excellent excuse to get out of the house.

The clinic waiting room bustled with departing and arriving patients, the noise at times reaching ear-splitting velocity as various animals elected to assert their individual authority and vie for supremacy.

It was well after five before she was able to leave, and in the house she went straight to the kitchen to prepare vegetables, then while waiting for the saucepans to boil she extracted veal slices for schnitzel from the refrigerator, then quickly set the table. There was sufficient soup to heat as a starter, and she quickly took a frozen fruit pie from the freezer and popped it into the oven. Within minutes everything was under control, and she literally ran towards the stairs with the intention of taking a record-quick shower. If she hurried, she could be ready in ten minutes.

Except that a solid muscular wall somehow got in the way somewhere between the dining-room and the foot of the stairs. 'Oh!'

Strong hands closed over her shoulders, steadied

and removed her to arms' length. 'Do you always run?' Jake demanded dryly, and she gave a wry smile.

'Not usually. Except when I'm in a hurry—like now.'

'Ah—I see. The boy-friend is due to arrive, and you have yet to make yourself beautiful,' he drawled sardonically.

Her gaze was remarkably direct. 'Why do you always resort to sarcasm?'

One eyebrow rose in quizzical amusement. 'Are you aggrieved because I implied you have to resort to cosmetics?'

'I don't stand in front of a mirror for hours studying my appearance,' Stephanie snapped, hating him afresh. 'If you don't mind?' she continued, giving him an arctic glare, then glanced pointedly to where his hands still grasped her arms.

'By all means,' he slanted mockingly, releasing her easily.

She moved past him, head held high, and as she reached the top of the stairs she hugged her arms across her midriff, aware of a strange tingling warmth where his hands had touched her skin. Her eyes closed momentarily. She must be going *mad*!

Jake Stanton was the epitome of everything she hated in a man—cynical, world-weary, and arrogant. Yet there was some magnetic pull of the senses, an elusive physical chemistry that could rob the breath from her throat and quicken her pulse—often both at the same time! It was almost as if some tiny devil was urging her to goad him in an effort to force a confrontation.

Suddenly she shivered. He was a million light

years ahead of her in just about everything. It showed in his eyes, the arrogant indolence he wore like a mantle, and undoubtedly countless women flocked around him like bees to a honey-pot. A cynical smile tugged the corners of her mouth. Word had already escaped that there was an attractive man in town—today the clinic's appointments had doubled! Yet honesty forced her to admit that he didn't deliberately cultivate an image. If anything, he counteracted an undoubted appeal with studied mockery, thus arousing an instinct to *hit* rather than kiss him!

Damn—this idle reflection wouldn't gain anything! She should be showered and slipping into fresh clothes instead of standing here daydreaming!

Ten minutes later she entered the kitchen, conducted a quick check of everything on the stove, then took bread rolls from the freezer and placed them ready to pop into the oven when needed. A cursory glance over the table ensured everything was as it should be, except for the carafe of wine chilling in the refrigerator, when the doorbell chimed.

Stephanie reached the hall just as Jake answered the door, and even from a relative distance she could sense Ian's composure had suffered a setback at the other man's appearance. Consequently her welcome was warmer than usual, although heaven knew what prompted her to reach up and bestow an affectionate kiss on Ian's cheek. Protectiveness, reassurance—she really didn't want to analyse it!

'Darling, let me introduce you,' she greeted with a smile. 'Jake Stanton—Ian Bryant.' Tucking her arm through Ian's, she urged him towards the lounge, aware of Jake's studied gaze and uncaring what connotations he placed on her actions. 'We've time for a drink first, or there's wine to go with the meal. Which would you prefer?'

'Oh, a drink,' Ian murmured abstractedly, then let his voice drop to a low undertone. 'He's making himself at home, isn't he? Answering the door as if he owns the place!'

'He was closest, that's all,' she soothed, then attempted brightly, 'How was your day?'

'The usual. Busy right through,' he responded without enthusiasm, and she inclined her head absently, knowing how much he disliked managing the family business. Selling books was far removed from his first love of mechanical engineering, yet being the only son, he had been thrust into managing the shop on his father's death over a year ago. Mrs Bryant helped out for a few hours each day, but Stephanie could appreciate how difficult it must be for him.

In the lounge she crossed to the drinks cabinet and poured his usual sherry, then handed him the glass. Jake, darn him, had followed them in, and politeness demanded she offer him something.

'Scotch, ice—no water,' he returned with urbanity, and the look she cast him would have quelled a lesser man. All it achieved was a raised eyebrow, then he lifted his glass and offered a mocking salute, 'Here's to health.'

Her own drink was an innocuous concoction which she sipped without testing, and suddenly aware of the acute silence, she rushed into speech with the first thing that entered her head.

'At least the rain has stopped.' Oh lord, she derided mentally, how inane! As a conversational gambit, the weather was low on the list of scintillating subjects!

'Have you heard from your father?' asked Ian, seemingly intent on ignoring the arresting man opposite, and Stephanie grasped the query as if it were a life-raft in a stormy sea.

'I received a cable this morning saying he'd arrived safely. He was going to phone, but I guess the time difference made it difficult.' Setting down her glass, she threw Jake a veiled glance, then excused herself on the pretext of dishing up the meal.

'Surely Mrs James is capable of doing that?' Ian intervened with a faint frown. 'She'll call us when it's ready.'

Here goes, Stephanie decided resignedly. Time to drop the bombshell! 'Mrs James is in hospital,' she revealed carefully. 'I've managed to find someone to take her place, and a Mrs Anderson is starting tomorrow.' She summoned a quick smile. 'Tonight's fare is hardly Cordon Bleu. Three minutes, okay?'

She could see a dozen questions forming on Ian's lips, but answering them right now was beyond her, and without further ado she crossed the room and closed the door quietly behind her.

In the kitchen she busied herself emptying the contents of saucepans into serving dishes, then carried them into the dining-room. A slow burning indignation put a fiery sparkle in her eyes. Damn Jake—he could at least try to enter the conversation!

She was just placing the soup tureen on the table when both men emerged from the hall, and one glance at Ian's set expression was enough to make her curse the older man afresh.

'Precisely where in Canada do you come from?' They were halfway through the soup when Ian voiced the query, and Jake directed him a level look.

'Vancouver.'

'Lived there all your life, I presume?'

Jake's eyes assumed a thoughtfulness as he regarded Stephanie, then he transferred his gaze to her companion. 'I spent the last ten years there,' he answered tolerantly.

'Jake's family live in Melbourne,' Stephanie put in.

'Are you married?'

'Am I obliged to answer that?'

She could sense the cynical amusement evident from the faint quirk of his lips, and could have slapped him. He wasn't lifting a finger to make things easy!

'But you can't lack for women friends,' Ian persisted with a temporary lapse of good manners in his quest for information, and she momentarily closed her eyes as she waited for the snub that must follow.

'Would it help if I were to produce a few?'

'I don't know what you mean,' Ian bristled, at a loss to match the other man's sophisticated adroitness.

'I think you do,' Jake responded softly.

With a strangled murmur Stephanie stood to her feet and removed the soup plates. In a minute she'd scream!

Somehow they got through the ensuing two courses, although at its end Stephanie wrote off the entire event as a total disaster. Neither man elected to speak further, and after a few hapless attempts she fell into an uneasy silence.

'I'll be at the clinic if any calls come through,' Jake informed her as he stood to his feet, then pushing in his chair he cast them both an enigmatic glance. 'Don't worry about coffee for me. I'll make some later.'

'As soon as I've cleared the kitchen I'm driving up to the hospital to see Mrs James,' she declared, uncaring whether Ian took her or not. The need to get out of the house was paramount.

'I'll leave the light on for you,' Jake drawled with hateful mockery, and it took all her self-control not to pick something up and throw it at him!

'Who the hell does he think he is?' Ian demanded wrathfully the instant the door closed, and Stephanie retorted with asperity,

'He knows exactly who he is. He's also the most impossible man I've ever met!'

It wasn't a successful evening. Even visiting Edith James did little to lift her flagging spirits, and afterwards fending Ian's relentless questions and observations almost brought her to the point of explosive anger.

Conversely, she refrained from telling him that Mrs Anderson was merely coming in for eight hours each day. He'd find out for himself soon enough, she decided darkly.

As the car drew to a halt outside the front entrance of the house, the ensuing silence between them could be cut with a proverbial knife.

'How about going to the cinema tomorrow night?'

Stephanie paused in reaching for the doorclasp and turned slightly in her seat. 'I'm not sure. Ring me tomorrow, okay?'

His hand fell on to her shoulder, its touch urgent as he tightened his grasp. 'Stephanie,' he muttered huskily, and she released an inaudible sigh.

'I'm tired,' she excused, loath to have him kiss her, and he groaned,

'Dammit, don't you understand? I'm torn apart just knowing he's in the same house with you. One has only to look at him to know he's a rake!'

'You met him for the first time tonight,' she offered quietly. 'How can you make such an observation after so brief an acquaintance?'

'You must find him attractive!' he burst out, and she slowly shook her head.

'Do you want me to say that I don't?'

'You *do*,' he accused. 'I knew it. You're just like all the rest!'

God give her patience, she prayed silently. 'You're overreacting.'

His eyes were full of glittering anger. 'Am I? I don't think so.'

'I've had about as much of this as I'm prepared to take,' she said tightly, moving to slide out from the passenger seat. Hard hands caught hold of her shoulders, pulling her backwards. 'Let me go, Ian.' Her voice was icy, and had no effect at all.

'I'm damned if I will,' he muttered thickly, twisting her round so he had easy access to her mouth.

His kiss was hard and unrestrained, as if he was bent on proving something—if only to himself. Then she was mercifully free, and she slid out from the car and slammed the door, uncaring as he revved the engine and took off at an alarming speed.

Her legs felt decidedly shaky as she moved to the front entrance, and to add to her chagrin she had trouble finding her key. At last her fingers encountered the slim piece of metal, and she slid it into the lock.

Safely inside, she closed the door behind her and secured the security chain.

'Well, well,' a deep voice drawled mockingly, 'you're home early.'

Stephanie turned to see Jake moving towards her, his entire stance reflecting sardonic amusement. Cold anger stirred her reflexes, making her want to lash out against him.

'Any reason why I shouldn't be?'

'None at all,' he murmured, his eyes narrowing slightly as they caught sight of her faintly swollen mouth. 'How did you find Mrs James?'

The last thing she wanted at this moment was polite conversation! 'As well as could be expected,' she said curtly, and deliberately moved past him towards the stairs. 'Goodnight.'

His monosyllabic response held a cynicism that made her want to turn and throw something, and only great restraint prevented a display of temper as without so much as a backward glance she ran quickly upstairs, and on gaining the sanctuary of her room she tossed her shoulderbag on to the bed with such force it bounced off and slithered across the floor.

CHAPTER THREE

THE following few days passed without mishap, the clinic becoming even more busy than before. Stephanie shortened her luncheon break in order to cope with the increasing influx, and began to adopt a firm stand over non-urgent appointments. Every eligible female, it seemed, wanted a legitimate excuse to confront the new man in town. On more than one occasion she stifled a growing cynicism over the effect Jake Stanton appeared to have on the feminine gender. From sixteen to sixty, few remained immune. Yet an inherent honesty forced her to admit that he didn't deliberately set out to charm. His approach was totally professional, polite, but little more than that. In one of her more analytical moments she deduced that it was his very professionalism that provided the challenge. Women wanted to find a chink in that sophisticated veneer and discover the man beneath the mask. She could have told each and every one of them that his armour was plated with tensile steel! Even living in the same house she was no closer to discovering what made him tick than any of her envious counterparts.

On the domestic front, Mrs Anderson was fast proving herself to be a veritable treasure. Not only was she more than adequate in the kitchen, she possessed a sunny nature and at times resorted to a wicked sense of humour that acted like a breath of fresh air.

Ian was something else. Twice when he rang she

had refused his invitation to go out, and his frustration in not being able to pin her down was becoming increasingly evident.

Halfway through dinner Friday evening the phone rang, and setting down her knife and fork Stephanie rose to her feet. 'I'll answer it.'

Expecting an emergency call, she registered surprise on hearing Ian's voice. 'Hi,' she greeted him with casual warmth. 'How are——'

'I think I'd better come over,' he began without preamble.

'Is something wrong?'

'That depends,' he answered, and a frown creased her brow at the tone of his voice.

'It's been a hectic week,' she offered quietly. 'I don't feel like going out.'

'Suits me fine. I'm on my way.'

'We're having dinner. Make it half an hour.'

She could sense him making an effort to control his temper. 'Don't dictate to me, Stephanie,' he warned emotively. 'I'm coming *now*.' The sound of the receiver being forcibly replaced made her wince.

'A personal call, I take it?' Jake observed mildly, and she cast him an angry glare as she returned to the table.

'Yes,' she conceded tightly.

'The boy-friend?'

'I doubt he'll retain that status for much longer,' she hinted darkly, regarding the contents on her plate with sudden lack of appetite.

'Ah,' he drawled sardonically. 'At a guess, the news of our replacement housekeeper not being resident has just filtered through.'

Stephanie shot him a wry glance. 'I'd say you've got it in one.'

'Shall I discreetly disappear when he arrives?'

'Why should you?' she managed evenly, and glimpsed his faint smile.

'Impossible to imagine you require my support.'

Her gaze was remarkably level. 'Somehow I don't see you in the role of mediator.' She drew a deep breath, then released it slowly. 'Unless I'm mistaken, the whole purpose of this sudden visit will have been instigated by Mrs Bryant.'

'An over-protective mother?'

'More than that,' she said dryly. 'I doubt there's a female on this earth who can measure up to her requirements for a prospective daughter-in-law.'

'She can't cling for ever.'

'No?'

They were about to start on dessert when the front doorbell pealed, and Stephanie restrained a faint grimace.

'That will be Ian.'

She ushered him into the lounge, and could hardly believe it when he insisted on joining her in the dining-room. 'Surely you can wait five minutes while we finish dinner?'

'We?' demanded Ian with scant regard for civility. 'You mean he's having dinner with you?'

Oh lord, this looked like turning out worse than she'd envisaged! 'What would you have me do, Ian?' she demanded with deceptive softness. 'Make him eat in his room each night?'

'I'm damned if I'll cool my heels in the lounge while you two closet yourselves together over a meal.' His voice bordered on belligerence, and she muttered beneath her breath as she followed him down the hall.

She was beginning to get angry, and if he didn't stop behaving in such a highhanded manner she'd tell him exactly what she thought of him—and his mother!

Jake looked up as Ian preceded her into the room, and his features bore an inscrutable expression as he greeted the younger man.

'You don't mind if we finish dessert?' Stephanie queried with deliberate emphasis as Ian pulled out a chair and sat down.

'I'll have some coffee,' he muttered.

'Why don't you make it?' she suggested sweetly. 'Perhaps Jake would like some, as well.'

'The kitchen isn't my domain,' Ian essayed with a scowl. 'I can wait until you've finished.'

Contrarily, she took over-long in eating her dessert, hardly tasting the delectable fruit. She was filled with an inner rage—with Ian for being a gullible fool in listening to his mother's bitter innuendoes.

Standing to her feet, she collected plates together and carried them through to the kitchen. Deliberately taking her time, she rinsed all the crockery and cutlery and stacked them into the dishwasher, then set to work on the saucepans. The kitchen restored to neatness, she plugged in the electric kettle and retrieved three mugs from the cupboard. Then she placed sugar, cream and milk on to a tray, added the steaming coffee pot and carried it through to the dining-room.

Presumably the two men had maintained some kind of conversation, although it was difficult to judge. Ian's face was set in faintly mutinous lines, almost to the point of an outright scowl, and Jake appeared blandly enigmatic.

Taking a seat, she distributed the mugs and sipped her coffee, endeavouring to draw a calming effect from the hot aromatic brew. Casting both men a quick encompassing glance she was struck by the difference between them. Not only physically, but in maturity. Beside Jake, Ian resembled an ill-mannered, spoilt little boy, and she marvelled that she hadn't recognised these qualities before.

'Come for a drive,' Ian insisted, not even bothering to ask. 'We need to talk.' He looked pointedly in Jake's direction, who to give credit, didn't appear a whit disturbed.

Don't lose your temper, she cautioned in self-admonition. Aloud, she refused quietly, 'We can talk in the lounge.'

'Anywhere in private.'

'If you'll excuse me?' Jake murmured sardonically, standing to his feet in one fluid movement. 'I'll be in the study. Your father offered me its use at any time, and there are some trade magazines I'd like to go through.' His gaze swept from Stephanie to Ian, and he gave the latter a curt nod. 'I'll take any incoming calls from there.'

'Did you have to be so insufferably rude?' Stephanie hissed the instant the door closed behind him, and Ian gave a careless shrug.

'It isn't his house.'

'It's not yours, either,' she was stung to retort, and a light tinge of colour crept into his face.

'What's all this I hear about your housekeeper?'

'Mrs Anderson?'

'Whatever her name is. Why doesn't she stay here?'

'Simply because she isn't able to,' she returned evenly, and he burst out,

'Well, someone should!'

'Why?'

'You can't be that stupid.'

'Thank you,' she said heavily. 'Personally, I think you're the one who's being ridiculous.'

'I don't care to have a hint of scandal attached to the reputation of the girl who might become my wife.'

This was even worse than she thought possible. 'There's no question of me becoming your wife,' she said with great restraint, when inwardly she was almost at boiling point. 'And I'm quite able to look after my own reputation.'

Ian looked momentarily lost for words. 'It just isn't good enough, Stephanie!'

'What, precisely?'

'Having him here without an adequate chaperone!'

'You sound like someone out of Emily Post! These are the eighties, not the Dark Ages.'

'That's all very well, but the two of you alone——'

'One of the most important factors in any relationship is trust,' she interrupted heatedly, standing to her feet. The look she cast him should have withered him on the spot. 'Something you don't appear to have. Now, if you don't mind, I'd like you to leave. In fact, I'm going to insist upon it. Before,' she said icily, 'we each say something we both may later regret.'

He seemed to be fighting an inner battle, then he capitulated with ill grace. 'I'll pick you up at seven tomorrow night.'

She looked at him solemnly, her eyes still dark with anger. 'I don't remember you asking me to go out.'

'Dammit, Stephanie,' he exploded, 'we usually go out on a Saturday night!'

'I'm sorry, but I've made other arrangements.' She hadn't—at least, not definitely. However, Karen, one of her close friends, had suggested they see a particularly good film that was showing at the local cinema. All it would take was a phone call, and she could do that as soon as Ian left.

'Stephanie!'

But she was already moving from the room, leaving him little option but to follow, and at the front door she bade him a perfunctory goodnight.

'I don't know what's come over you,' he muttered, pausing hesitantly. 'You've changed.'

It had to be for the better, she told herself silently.

'I'll call you tomorrow.'

She gave a careless shrug. 'That's up to you.'

He looked as if he was about to kiss her, then obviously decided against it.

After locking the door she crossed into the lounge and switched on the television, then sat down to watch a locally-produced programme. When that finished she changed channels and viewed a half-hour comedy. There had been no sign or sound of Jake, and she concluded that he must still be in the study. Deciding she didn't care where he was, she doused the lights and went upstairs to bed.

Saturday morning's clinic was suitably busy. Even Michael, usually a tireless worker, complained *sotto voce* as it drew near lunchtime.

'Going out tonight?'

He asked the same question every week, but ever hopeful he refused to give up in case she might relent.

'I am,' Stephanie grinned, and caught a glimpse of resignation in his expression. 'With Karen.'

His eyebrows shot upwards. 'Hmm, that's a change. Don't tell me Ian is on the way out—at last?'

'And if he is?'

His smile broadened cheekily. 'I'm next in line.'

'Says who?' she retaliated, enjoying the light bantering they invariably exchanged.

'A very good authority—me.'

'Oh, Michael!' she remonstrated laughingly, and he grinned back, unabashed.

'Oh, *Michael*,' he mimicked without rancour. 'When will you begin to take me seriously?'

'I've never thought of you in that way,' she explained gently, and glimpsed his cynical smile.

'I know,' he acknowledged wryly.

The telephone saved her from having to comment, and it was after one o'clock when she eventually locked the outer door and a further ten minutes before she had restored the reception desk to order. By then Michael had left, and only Jake remained tidying up the surgery.

Stephanie ran a cursory check, switched the phone over to the house, then indicated her intention to leave. 'Lunch in about thirty minutes, okay?'

His response was curtly monosyllabic and she suppressed a grimace as she made her way towards the house. The weekend stretched ahead, and she intended to be out as much as possible. Remaining in his company for anything unrelated to necessity was unthinkable!

As it turned out, she needn't have worried, for after lunch Jake mentioned that he would be leaving for Melbourne early the following morning and wouldn't be back until late.

The evening was scarcely memorable, but

Karen's company provided some essential light relief, and the film was excellent.

Monday dawned with the promise of rain, added to which was a fall in temperature that whipped ice into the wind and sent Stephanie switching on the central heating both in the house and the clinic.

Armed with a long list of required provisions, she set off into town shortly after midday, and after parking her car she moved through the automatic doors and selected a trolley.

The supermarket was full, and Stephanie suppressed a feeling of irritation that she'd chosen this particular time to do her weekly shopping. Not that she had much choice, really, for the clinic had been unusually busy and taking time off was practically an impossibility.

At least now they had a daily help, which ensured that the house was smoothly run. A slight grimace creased her pleasant features. If the present influx of patients kept up, she'd have to think seriously about enlisting some part-time help in the clinic itself.

'Stephanie, how nice to see you!'

She came out of her reverie with a slight jolt, recognising a familiar voice. 'Mrs Bryant, how are you?' she greeted politely, summoning a faint smile, and saw the slight narrowing of the other woman's expression.

'My dear, I've been meaning to call you—for a chat.' Her lips pursed. 'You no longer have your own dear mother to guide you, I know, but with your father absent someone should offer some advice.'

Oh lord! Stephanie groaned. I really don't have time for this. 'Perhaps later?' she prevaricated.

'I've only an hour in which to complete my shopping, and there are a few other things I must do before getting back to the clinic.'

Mrs Bryant's facial muscles tightened into an uncompromising mask. 'In is quite besotted with you, but we both take a very dim view of your present predicament. It simply isn't within the bounds of decency to have that man sleeping in the same house.'

It said much for Stephanie's innate good manners that she didn't explode, and she endeavoured to dampen down the anger that rose to the fore, forcing herself to speak with a calmness she was far from feeling. 'I'm sure Ian has told you that every effort has been made to find a live-in housekeeper,' she managed quietly.

'Well, something should be done,' Mrs Bryant declared with bristling righteousness. 'It isn't seemly for a young woman to be living alone with a man in the same house.'

Careful, Stephanie cautioned. 'If you're so concerned, perhaps you can think of a solution?'

'Why not move in with one of your girl friends until your father returns?'

She drew a deep breath. 'Why should I impose on others when there's no need?' she parried, and watched as the other woman drew herself up to her full height.

'No need?' Narrow lips tightened into a thin line, and pale blue eyes became cold. 'What of your reputation? Ian deserves a girl whose morals are beyond reproach.'

'Are you suggesting mine are not?'

'Well, my dear, who knows what temptations stand in your way in the present circumstances?'

That did it. 'You possess a devious mind, Mrs

Bryant,' Stephanie declared with sweet civility, 'which would be better employed than with something that's none of your business.' Without waiting to see the registered shock, she pushed her trolley forward and consulting her list, added to her purchases until her shopping was completed.

The various brown paper bags stowed in the boot of her Datsun, she walked across the parking area to the street and crossed it to go into the bank. Business completed, she collected the few necessities remaining on her list, then moved back to the car.

Driving home she became consumed with ill-concealed rage, so that by the time she parked the car she was incapable of rational speech.

Jake walked into the kitchen just as she deposited the last of the packages on to the table, and the look she threw him would have quelled a lesser man on the spot. As it was, he raised an enquiring eyebrow and queried with cynical mockery,

'What's bitten you?'

'A procrastinating queen bee!' she vented waspishly, and it was only by exercising considerable restraint that she didn't actually *throw* the can of asparagus she held in her hand at his hatefully amused countenance.

'My, my,' he drawled, and pulling one of the packages towards him he began to unpack its contents. 'I take it you returned the sting?'

She threw him a wrathful glare. 'You can be sure of it!'

'Have you had lunch?'

'No. I haven't time—what's more, it would stick in my throat!'

'Care to elaborate?'

'You'd laugh.'

His glance was remarkably steady. 'You didn't.'

'I don't possess your sophisticated sense of humour.'

'Maybe you should cultivate it.'

She flashed him a wry look. 'Mrs Bryant needs the lesson, not me.'

'Ah, I see.'

'Do you?' she demanded sceptically.

'Oh, yes,' Jake opined sardonically. 'Concern has been expressed at her prospective daughter-in-law sleeping unchaperoned under the same roof as an eligible man.'

Stephanie lifted her head and regarded him levelly. 'Are you? Eligible, I mean?'

'Question and answer time?'

'My father obviously thought you above reproach, but he neglected to reveal any real information.'

His mouth slanted in open mockery. 'Is it important?'

She managed a careless shrug and began stowing the groceries on to the pantry shelves. 'Not really. In little more than three weeks you'll leave our orbit and will probably never be seen or heard of by any of us again.'

His expression assumed an inscrutability that was impossible to penetrate. 'There's some soup left. I'll put it on to heat.'

She shot him a dark glance. 'I really don't want it.'

'But you'll have it, just the same.'

'Are you always this bossy?' she demanded crossly.

'When I consider it necessary.'

'I'm not a child to be ordered around! Anyway, aren't you due back at the clinic?'

'Now who's being bossy?'

A sigh of resignation left her lips. 'All right, I'll have the darn soup. I'll even grab a few cracker biscuits or some bread to have with it. Now, will you please get off my back?'

He lifted his hands in a gesture of mock surrender. 'I'm on my way. Incidentally, I won't be in for dinner.'

'A date? My goodness!' Her eyebrows lifted with amusement. 'Which particular patient's owner is the lucky woman?'

'None,' Jake returned smoothly. 'I'll leave a number where I can be contacted in case of an emergency.' With easy lithe strides he moved towards the door, and she watched his tall frame disappear out of sight.

The afternoon passed without mishap, and by adroit management they were able to keep their appointments on time, closing the clinic doors after the last patient at five-thirty.

Mrs Anderson had left a meal warming in the oven, and Stephanie removed the dish, her tastebuds quivering with hunger at the delicious aroma pervading the kitchen. Jake had disappeared upstairs, presumably to shower and change, and she wasted little time in collecting cutlery and a plate for herself.

She was halfway through the tasty steak and kidney pie when the phone rang, and she crossed to pick up the receiver, automatically making a professional response, hoping it wasn't an emergency call.

'Stephanie?'

'Hello, Ian,' she murmured cautiously.

'Would you like to visit Frank and Thelma? They're viewing a few movies on video, one of which is that film which scooped all the Oscars this year.'

There were letters she should write, a few phone calls, but nothing that couldn't wait. Besides, she didn't fancy spending the evening alone. 'Why not?' she acquiesced lightly.

'I'll pick you up in an hour.'

She was ascending the stairs when she met Jake on his way down.

'Going out?'

'Yes, with Ian,' she told him, meeting his slightly narrowed gaze. 'I'll switch on the answerphone before I leave.'

'I expect to be back around eleven.'

'I'll leave the outside light on. You've got Dad's set of keys, haven't you?'

His curt nod ended their exchange, and she reached the top of the stairs as the front door closed behind him.

A quick shower restored her spirits, then changing into slacks and a jumper she ran a brush through her hair, applied a minimum amount of make-up, then slipped her feet into slim-heeled shoes and caught up her shoulderbag, switched off her bedroom light and moved downstairs.

Ian arrived five minutes later, and she flipped the switch for the answerphone, then went out to meet him.

They went straight out to the car, and during the five-minute drive he scarcely said a word, answering her light queries perfunctorily, so that she was on the verge of demanding a reason for his bearish behaviour when he brought the vehicle to a halt in Frank's driveway.

After being led indoors, Thelma plied them with coffee while her husband set up the video recorder, then silence reigned as they gave their undivided attention to the images on screen.

It was ten o'clock when they left, and Stephanie could sense Ian was conducting an inner struggle, undecided whether to pursue an issue undoubtedly instigated by his mother's harassed nagging.

'You'd better get it off your chest,' she said quietly as he stopped the car adjacent the house.

'Dammit, Stephanie,' he began explosively, 'why do you persist in staying alone with him?'

'Do we really have to go over this all over again?' she queried hollowly, turning slightly in her seat to face him.

'Don't my wishes count for anything?'

'Is your opinion of me so—precarious?'

'Allowing things to continue will only put temptation in your way,' he insisted doggedly.

'Supposing I were to find Jake attractive?' she offered with seeming deliberation. 'The feeling would have to be reciprocated. Where do you imagine that would lead? Bearing in mind that our respective fathers are not only fellow associates, but also friends.'

Ian's laugh totally lacked any semblance of humour. 'You only have to take one look at him,' he declared derisively. 'He's a womaniser, a rake. It's only a matter of time.'

Stephanie became still. 'What's only a matter of time?'

'Oh, come on. I don't believe you're that green!'

Very carefully she said, 'Exactly what are you insinuating?'

'Bed,' he elaborated bluntly. 'Yours, or his—it's all the same. One way or another, that's where you'll end up.'

'Thanks for your trust,' she answered slowly. 'It

wouldn't occur to you to shut your ears to the vindictive suggestions your mother has voiced, would it? You've known me all my life, been aware of my views on just about everything, yet suddenly I've become a scarlet woman.' She reached for the doorclasp. 'I was prepared to ignore your mother's rudeness, but coupled with yours, I find I really can't. I think it's best if we don't see each other again.'

'I love you,' he bit out in anguish, and she slowly shook her head.

'Not enough, it would seem.'

'Stephanie——'

'Goodbye, Ian.'

'I won't let you go,' he said thickly, reaching for her and pulling her into his arms. His mouth sought hers with a desperate hunger, his hands hard on her arms as he sought to enforce his strength.

She began to struggle, evading his mouth as it moved hotly over her face. 'Leave me alone!'

'No. I'll have you first, I swear it!'

'At least be man enough to retain some civility,' she insisted, endeavouring to slip out of his grasp.

'Man enough? I'll show you how much of a man I really am!'

His hands slid beneath her jumper and clutched hold of her breasts, crushing them painfully, then his mouth was on hers, stifling the outrage that rose to her lips.

This sort of behaviour was so alien to his character that it took a few seconds for her to assimilate his intention, and when it became clear he wasn't about to desist she began hitting him, struggling with increasing fervour to be free of him. His strength outmatched hers, his fingers tearing at the fastening of her bra, hurting her in his effort to free her breasts of the confining silk and lace.

With a sense of desperation she fought to be free of him, then gave a groan of despair when she realised her struggles had only aided in allowing him to pull her jumper upwards to form a makeshift restriction confining her arms. For a moment she thought she might suffocate, then she let out a muffled scream as she felt his teeth close roughly over one vulnerable nipple. Not content, he nibbled its twin, nipping painfully whenever it pleased him, then he began a similar assault beneath each roseate peak, sending shocks of pain through her body as he bruised the tender flesh.

No matter how she twisted and turned she couldn't free her arms from his steel-like grasp, and the entire proceedings began to take on nightmarish proportion. She tried talking to him, rationalising, her voice sounding indistinct and muffled as the woollen garment hugged her face.

Then suddenly Ian stilled, and in that moment she was able to wrench her hands free, letting her arms down and mercifully removing the claustrophobic jumper from her face.

For a split second Stephanie thought her pleadings had finally reached him, then she became aware of an illumination as car lights drew increasingly nearer in the distance.

It could only be Jake returning home, and she acted on impulse, reaching for the doorclasp, and moving with fear-induced speed. If she could get indoors before Jake garaged his car, she could be upstairs and safely into her room before he entered the house.

She was free, out of the car and running, aware

that Ian had started the engine and was as intent on leaving the scene with equal rapidity, judging from the faint squeal of tyres as they spun on the loose-metalled driveway.

Her fingers were shaky as they opened her bag and searched fruitlessly for the key, then finally they recognised the hard metal object, and she extracted it with a prayer of thankfulness just as the Lamborghini swept to a halt before the closed garage doors.

She'd make it with only seconds to spare, and even as she closed the front door behind her she heard the solid muffled thud as the garage door shut, then without waiting she flew up the stairs.

In her room she leaned back against the closed door and drew in great gulping breaths in an attempt to bring some semblance of calm to her ragged nerves. Slowly she closed her eyes, then re-opened them as the events of the past half hour flooded through her brain in horrifying kaleido-scopic sequence.

Stephanie had no idea how long she remained leaning against the door. It could have been scant minutes, or more than twenty—she really had no recollection. Slowly a sense of normality began to return, and with it came anger. Her skin felt unclean—her whole body, and she moved about the room collecting her nightwear and dressing-gown. The need to remove every trace of Ian's lust-induced mouth and hands was all-consuming, and in the bathroom she eyed the bath with favour, electing to fill the capacious tub almost to the brim. Scented foam covered its entire surface, and she quickly stepped in and lay down until only her head was visible.

Slowly the heated water began to have a

relaxing effect, soothing her body, although her thoughts were far removed from tranquillity! Even now she found it difficult to assimilate Ian's horrific mood-swing. She'd known him all through schooldays, played tennis and squash with him at the local clubs, attended social functions, and for the past year they had developed a deeper friendship to a point where both accepted their relationship might lead to something permanent. Suddenly she shivered. To have imagined Ian might possess a dark side to his character was something she hadn't even contemplated.

A sudden double knock almost succeeded in jack-knifing her from the bath, and of their own volition her arms crossed protectively across her breasts.

'Stephanie, have you fallen asleep?' Jake demanded brusquely. 'You've been in there almost an hour!'

'I'm fine,' she assured him in a faintly strangled voice, standing to her feet at once. Reaching out, she grasped hold of a towel and wrapped it round her, then pulled the plug, releasing the water.

'I'm reassured to hear it,' he drawled, cynicism uppermost.

Oh, he really was the limit! 'I frequently take long baths late at night,' she managed with evident sarcasm.

'Perhaps you could curtail the habit—at least while I'm in residence? I couldn't bear to be held responsible for your drowning,' he added sardonically, and she was moved to retort,

'I'll pen a note exonerating you of any blame should such a catastrophe occur!'

'Goodnight, Stephanie,' he declared mockingly, and she didn't bother returning his salutation.

Towelled dry, she donned her pyjamas and shrugged her arms into the warm wrap, then caught up her clothes and made her way back to the bedroom.

There was a thin thread of light showing beneath Jake's door, and she silently wished him as sleepless a night as he deserved! Then she suddenly sobered as realisation dawned. If it hadn't been for his timely arrival ... A deep shudder shook her slim body. It didn't pay to think about what the consequences might have been.

With considerable fortitude she entered her room and closed the door, switched off the light and slid into bed.

Sleep refused to grant its blissful oblivion, and she tossed and turned, plumped her pillow more times than she cared to count until finally she slid out from beneath the covers in angry desperation. Her nerves were as taut as a tightly-stretched wire, and her head felt as if tiny hammers were banging away in strident discord. There had to be something to help her sleep—Paracetamol, Disprin; even something stronger.

Pulling on her wrap, she moved silently down the hall to the bathroom, and after a few minutes she came up with an empty foil strip at the back of the only drawer likely to hold such medication.

Damn! Now she'd have to go downstairs.

Suiting thought to action, she padded towards the stairs, her bare feet making no sound on the carpet. She didn't bother switching on any lights until she reached the kitchen, and with the ease of familiarity she opened the appropriate cupboard and extracted the necessary tablets.

What she needed was a stiff brandy, she

grimaced with retrospect. Or maybe *two*. At least then she could collapse into bed in a heap and let the alcohol take effect!

Tablets in hand, she moved through to the lounge and crossed to the drinks cabinet. Selecting a glass, she poured a generous measure of brandy and took a tentative sip, grimacing as the neat spirit burnt the back of her throat. How could anyone profess to like such a vile taste? Even with ice there was no measurable improvement. There was some ginger ale which should successfully dilute it, and after adding some she had to concede that the contents of her glass were more palatable. So much so, she poured another.

'Well, well,' a cynical voice drawled, 'what have we here?'

Stephanie slowly turned, letting her eyes swing up to encompass his dark inscrutable gaze before sliding down to rest on his mouth. It was a very— oh, what was the word for it? *Sensual*, she decided after a seemingly endless deliberation. Wondering how those lips would feel on hers set up an irregular tattoo in the region of her breast that all too quickly seemed to reverberate in the pulse at her throat. Her temples began to throb, and she actually felt a slow delicious ache begin in the pit of her stomach. The brandy must be infinitely more potent than she thought!

'I couldn't sleep,' she enunciated carefully, then wondered why she felt the necessity to speak so slowly. 'What are you doing up? I thought you'd gone to bed.'

His eyes narrowed fractionally. 'I had.'

'So why are you here?'

'I heard someone moving around and felt I should investigate.'

She raised the glass in a mock salute. 'You can relax—I'm no burglar.'

'So I see.'

'Do you really?' she retorted deliberately, and saw the edge of his mouth lift with sardonic amusement.

'I think you should go back to bed.'

'Oh, I will. Just as soon as I've finished this drink.'

'*Now*, Stephanie,' he inclined softly, with just a hint of steel, and she laughed.

'My, my! Are you usually so masterful?'

He took the few steps forward necessary to bring him within touching distance. 'Come on, there's a good girl, hmm?'

She smiled, a slow wistful smile that held, if she did but know it, infinite pathos. 'I really need the effect this will have.'

'That bad?'

Her eyes widened. 'You can't know.'

'The best part of an argument is making up,' he told her with a lopsided smile. 'Young Bryant will undoubtedly be on the phone before breakfast begging forgiveness.'

She eyed him carefully. 'He won't, and—I won't. Forgive him—ever,' she declared slowly.

'Finish your drink,' Jake instructed quietly. 'Then I'll see you upstairs.'

'Good idea.' She lifted the glass and tossed back the remaining contents with considerable panache, then spoilt everything by giving an unladylike hiccup. 'I think——' she didn't wait to finish, and with a groan she moved past him and broke into a run, just reaching the downstairs bathroom in time to be wretchedly ill.

Afterwards she washed her face and cleaned her

teeth, then lifted shaky fingers to brush back the
hair from her face.

'Are you all right?'

She hadn't heard a thing, and she jerked with
surprise at the sound of Jake's voice so close behind.

Was she? Certainly she felt better, physically, but
her emotions were torn to shreds. For some idiotic
reason she felt like crying, but to resort to feminine
tears now would be the ultimate humiliation. It took
considerable bravado to raise her eyes to meet his,
but she managed it. 'I'll survive.'

His eyes became hard, and far more discerning
than she wanted. 'Suppose you tell me what
happened?'

Her nerves screamed in angry rejection. 'I'd like
to go to bed.'

A hand reached out and took hold of her chin,
lifting it high as he examined the delicate planes of
her face, the dark hollows beneath her eyes, the
long-fringed lashes veiling her expression.

'My headlights picked you out as I came up the
drive, running from Bryant's car like someone
possessed, then Bryant took off with more speed
than care.'

Her eyes closed for a few mere seconds, then
slowly opened. 'What do you want, Jake? A blow-
by-blow account?'

The imprecation he muttered brought a rush of
colour to her cheeks, but he offered no apology.

After a long time she said quietly, 'I'm all
right—really.' For some reason she couldn't look
away, and with mesmerised fascination she let her
eyes widen fractionally to meet his intent gaze,
glimpsing some indefinable emotion in those hard
brown eyes that was successfully masked within
seconds by sardonic cynicism, and she swallowed

convulsively as she struggled to summon her voice.
'It's late,' she managed evenly, moving to one side
so that she could pass him. 'Goodnight.'

He didn't say a word, and she could feel his eyes
following her all the way down the hall until she
reached the stairs. By the time she reached her
room the entire length of her spine was tingling,
and as she closed the door behind her it took every
ounce of resolve not to burst into ignominious
tears.

Slowly she crossed to her bed and slid in
between the covers, then reached up and switched
off the lamp.

CHAPTER FOUR

'JAKE STANTON, please.'

The voice was melodious, its trans-Atlantic accent huskily attractive, and Stephanie felt her fingers instinctively tighten on the receiver.

'Mr Stanton is in surgery,' she told him. 'Can I help you?'

'What time will he be finished?'

'The last appointment is at five o'clock.'

'Thank you.'

The line went dead, and Stephanie slowly replaced the receiver. No ordinary caller, she perceived, and unless she was mistaken, not the owner of a prospective patient. Her imagination ran riot, wondering if the projected image matched up to the voice.

It wasn't long before she discovered that it did. At exactly five the door slid open and a vision of sheer beauty entered the waiting room.

Tall and willowy, attired in the latest fashion from the tips of her Italian-made shoes to the signature scarf knotted carelessly at her neck, her burnished auburn hair perfectly groomed, she swept towards reception in a cloud of exotically expensive and instantly recognisable perfume.

A red Irish Setter reared up from its lolling position at its master's feet, nose quivering, ears and tail alert, to subside seconds later with a pitiful whine. The only other animal occupant, a seal-point Siamese, lifted its head to ascertain if there was any immediate threat, then maintained an unblinking surveillance.

Stephanie looked at the perfectly made-up face and immediately became aware of her own shortcomings by comparison. She didn't need to look in a mirror to see that she'd retained only a tinge of lipstick, the thin film of powder over her nose had disappeared, and that her hair had resorted to a riot of curls.

'Can I be of any assistance?'

A slow curving smile widened the skilfully painted mouth. 'I doubt it,' she drawled with a seductive laugh. 'Will I disrupt things too much if I wait here for Jake?'

It had to be *Jake*, Stephanie thought silently, wondering at her own stupidity in surmising otherwise. Aloud she murmured, 'By all means take a seat.'

Five minutes later Michael ushered out a patient and its owner, picked up the next file from Stephanie's desk, then glanced across the room. His expression was comical for the scant second it took him to successfully mask it, and the look he cast Stephanie was positively dazed.

It would be interesting to see how Jake handled the appearance of his—*friend*? The descriptive was far too tame. Such self-assurance only came with the knowledge of infinite possession.

The waiting room gradually emptied, and as the last patient retreated from the clinic's waiting room Stephanie felt her eyes drawn towards the surgery door. Michael emerged and bade her goodnight, then a familiar broad frame filled the aperture, and she almost held her breath as his gaze skimmed across to the woman seated on the far side of the room.

There was no surprise evident, not even a flicker

of emotion on those dark saturnine features. Looking at him, Stephanie could hardly believe he could appear so unmoved.

His hands pushed into the pockets of his trousers, and his stance took on a peculiar stillness, rather like that of a jungle animal assessing an unknown entity.

'Hello, Jake.' Every movement was elegance personified as she rose to her feet, and she stood waiting, a soft hesitant smile parting her lips.

'Alana.' The acknowledgment bore finely-edged mockery, and Stephanie was aware that she was suddenly an unwanted spectator.

'If you'll excuse me?'

Jake spared her a swift enigmatic glance. 'I'll lock up.'

Stephanie placed the cover over her typewriter, then proffered a slight smile that was meant to encompass them both, but probably went unnoticed. Certainly it wasn't acknowledged, and she moved towards the door with a sense of unreality, almost as if she were detached from the scene.

The few dozen steps separating the clinic from the house had never taken so long, and once indoors she moved to the kitchen where she automatically checked the meal Mrs Anderson had prepared, then went about setting the table.

Fool, she scolded silently. Jake wouldn't be eating in tonight. Not with that vision of loveliness his willing supplicant.

Who was she? Girl-friend? Lover? Fiancée? Surely not *wife*? It didn't take much imagination to deduce she'd followed him here.

Damn. It was none of her business. Why should she care, anyway?

Suddenly cross with herself she moved back to

the kitchen and plugged in the electric kettle. A cup of coffee would do much to restore a modicum of common sense.

She had just finished it when she heard the side door close, and she looked up as Jake entered the room.

'I'll be away for a few hours,' he told her without preamble. 'No dinner—I'll eat out.'

What could she say? What right did she have to say *anything*? At that precise moment even a single word would have stuck in her throat.

Afterwards she served up a solitary meal and spent ten minutes forking the contents around her plate, eating little more than a mouthful or two.

She couldn't concentrate on anything, and even a favourite television programme failed to capture her interest. At eleven she locked up, switched on the outside light, then climbed the stairs to her room.

In bed she turned the pages of a book without reading so much as a line, then placed it on the pedestal and determinedly switched off the lamp. Endeavouring to relax in order to summon an envied somnolent state proved hopeless and she tossed and turned, even resorted to counting sheep, without success.

It was late when Jake returned, very late. Two-thirty-five, to be precise. The powerful beam of the Lamborghini's headlights illuminated her room as it swept up the drive, and in the still night air Stephanie heard the faint clunk of the car door closing, and sensed rather than heard him enter the house.

Breakfast was a strained meal. Stephanie couldn't think of one sensible topic of conversation, and escaped the instant she finished her coffee. If Jake noticed her discomfiture he gave no sign. He didn't even *look* tired, damn him, she decided peevishly. She was nursing a headache, and worse, a strange ache in the region of her heart.

It was mid-afternoon when Stephanie took that fateful phone call, and she recognised the faintly husky, feminine voice at once.

'I'd like to speak to Jake, please.'

'He's attending a patient at the moment,' Stephanie explained carefully. 'Can I have him call you?'

Silence echoed down the line for a few seemingly long seconds. 'Ask him to phone his wife. He has the number.' Then the line went dead.

Wife? A hundred different thoughts vied for supremacy, and none made any sense. There was nothing to be gained from Jake's expression when she relayed the message, for he merely gave a curt nod in acquiescence.

He missed dinner again, and returned equally late. It gave Stephanie a small dart of satisfaction to glimpse the faint edge of weariness tinging his broad-chiselled profile as he ate breakfast.

'If there are any personal calls for me, take a message,' Jake slanted as she excused herself from the table, and she looked at him in surprise.

'Very well,' she answered stiltedly.

It required all Stephanie's skilled tactfulness to deal with the beautiful Alana when she rang, not once, but twice during the course of the day, and it was really no surprise at all when she swept into the clinic's waiting room a few minutes before five.

Looking like something out of *Vogue*, Alana Stanton spared Stephanie a slight smile before taking a seat. She didn't have long to wait, for a minor miracle had occurred in that their list of appointments had kept surprisingly to the scheduled timetable with no emergencies to provide a disruptive factor.

Michael took one glance at the almost empty waiting room, then swung his expressive gaze towards Stephanie. 'I'm off, see you in the morning.'

Jake appeared within minutes, and there was no mistaking the slight tensing of his jaw as Alana rose to greet him.

'Darling—I thought I'd surprise you,' she effused with sparkling warmth, and her eyes moved towards Stephanie in silent query.

Taking the cue, Stephanie quickly placed the cover over her typewriter and uttered a slightly strangled 'goodnight'.

'I need some files,' declared Jake, turning slightly, and she had a difficult time controlling her surprise.

'Yes, of course.' She endeavoured to keep her voice even as she moved towards the large set of filing drawers. 'If you'll tell me which ones, I'll get them.'

'Oh, Jake,' Alana protested with soft remonstrance, 'you're not working late, are you? I thought we'd go somewhere for dinner. We have so much to talk about.'

His eyes bore a remoteness that was chilling. 'We did all the talking necessary last night. Now, if you'll excuse me?'

Stephanie couldn't believe her ears, and only quick reflexes saved her from catching her fingers in the heavy filing drawer.

'Jake, I drove down especially!' Alana protested.

'Then you should have saved yourself the trip.' He took a few steps towards the reception desk, and his features were devoid of any expression as he checked the following morning's appointments in the book. 'Robinson, Sullivan and Peters,' he indicated. 'Bring them in, and don't bother switching the phone over to the house. I have a few calls to make first.'

The atmosphere was so electric Stephanie hardly dared draw breath, and she watched with mesmerised fascination as Alana reached out and placed a perfectly manicured hand on his sleeve.

'Jake—please!'

There was a flicker of emotion visible as he looked down at the fingers resting on his arm, then very carefully he removed them. 'Go home, Alana,' he said quietly.

'Can't we talk alone?'

'To what end?' He turned towards Stephanie. 'I need your assistance here for half an hour. Dinner can wait.'

'You're having dinner with her?' Alana demanded incredulously.

'Yes.'

'At the house?'

'Why not?' he drawled sardonically, his expression becoming ruthlessly implacable. 'It's where we both stay.'

'You're living there—*together*?' Alana queried, her eyes narrowing speculatively as she swung her attention towards Stephanie. 'I don't believe it!'

'It happens to be a fact,' Jake assured her silkily.

The other woman gave a sharp intake of breath. 'Obviously you've taken leave of your senses.'

She could be right, if it were true, Stephanie thought wryly. Jake possessed an arresting masculinity, which coupled with rugged good looks, ensured that he would always have his pick of women. Why, when he could have someone as lovely as the beautiful Alana, would he elect to give his attention to *her*? If it wasn't so ludicrous it could almost be funny.

'You think so?' he asked deliberately.

'How can you be so heartless?' Alana pleaded, and there was a shimmer of tears clouding those beautiful eyes as she gazed beseechingly at him.

'Go back to Melbourne, Alana,' he directed quietly. 'If you've any sense, you'll catch the next plane home to the States.' Without a word he picked up the files Stephanie had placed on the desk, then turned towards the surgery. 'Stephanie?'

'Jake!'

His gaze was totally merciless. 'Goodbye, Alana.'

'I won't give you up—I can't!'

'We're divorced—remember?'

Stephanie suddenly had trouble with her breathing.

'I made a mistake,' Alana cried, stricken, and his expression became wholly cynical.

'It's too late.'

'I don't believe that!'

'If you don't leave now,' Jake declared in a dangerously soft voice, 'I'll have no choice but to have you forcibly removed from the premises. I'm sure you want that even less than I do.'

'All right, I'll go.' Her eyes suddenly became hard and glittery. 'But I'll be back. What's more, I can promise you haven't heard the last of me!'

Stephanie watched in mesmerised fascination as the older woman turned and swept out the door, and within seconds an engine roared to life, then leapt down the driveway with a spurt of flying metal and squealing tyres.

Almost as if the past ten minutes had never been, Jake moved towards the surgery. 'Shall we dispense with work?'

'As you disposed of your ex-wife?' The words were out before she could halt them, and she experienced inexplicable fear as his eyes hardened with an icy rage.

'That's none of your business.'

'I know,' she admitted without remorse. 'But you were unnecessarily cruel in letting her assume we share more than the house.'

'You didn't deny it.'

'My God,' she whispered, her eyes wide, 'you despicable—bastard! If you think I actually enjoyed being an unwanted spectator in that vitriolic little scene, you have to be mad!' Her eyes sparkled with temper. 'You deliberately used me, and I find that unforgivable!'

'Stephanie,' he warned hardily. 'Let's go over those files, shall we?'

She could easily have hit him. 'Damn you! Do it yourself!' Uncaring, she walked past him, intent on escaping, and almost gasped as hard hands closed over her arms effectively bringing her to a halt. She looked up, then wished she hadn't.

Cold anger emanated from every muscle and sinew. His jaw was tight with it, and his eyes were inimical brown chips as he gazed at her. 'I don't need self-righteous feminine indignation,' he bit out.

'What *do* you need?' she demanded contemptuously, then the scream that rose in her throat never found voice as his mouth closed down over hers.

It couldn't by the wildest stretch of imagination be called a kiss, part of her brain registered numbly as he subjected her lips to a punishingly brutal assault, plundering until the delicate skin became grazed and split. Just as she thought she could bear no more he lifted his head and thrust her to arms' length.

Stephanie almost fell, and would have if he hadn't supported her. She felt numb, her jaw and mouth so sore she doubted her ability to speak. Even her limbs weren't her own, refusing to obey the demands of her brain to turn and run—as far and as fast as her legs would carry her.

Quite what might have happened next remained unknown as the shrill peal of the telephone broke the stillness of the room, and with a muttered oath Jake leant forward and plucked the receiver from its rest.

Stephanie heard his voice, but for those infinitesimal seconds nothing seemed to register. Her entire body appeared to be in shock, and she looked at him dazedly when he held the receiver towards her.

'It's for you.'

There wasn't a flicker of emotion in his voice, nor any visible sign of regret to be evidenced from his expression, and with a strangled sound she took the receiver from his hand, taking great care that her fingers didn't come into contact with his.

For a moment she failed to recognise the caller, then a sense of normality rose to the surface and with it came a measure of control as she found herself answering, 'Yes, I'm fine. The movies? Tonight? No, I'm not doing anything, and yes, I'd love to come.' It was a blessing in disguise, she decided shakily as she made arrangements to meet Karen in town. To have stayed in the house for the evening would have been impossible.

'You're going out?' Jake queried brusquely, his expression enigmatic, and she fixed her gaze on a point near his right shoulder.

'Yes.'

'Dinner?'

She lifted her head slightly and met his penetrating gaze. The invitation hadn't included a meal, but the thought of food, especially the eating of it in his presence, almost made her ill. 'I'm sure you can manage on your own,' she said stiffly, moving past him towards the door.

In the house she swiftly showered and dressed, then satisfied with her appearance she ran quickly downstairs to her car. There was no sign of Jake, and she told herself fiercely that she didn't care a jot whether he ate alone—or even if he ate at all.

Karen's vivacity acted like a soothing balm, and for the space of four hours Stephanie managed to dismiss Jake to the deep recess of her mind.

It was only when she was driving home that his image rose to taunt her, and the memory of that punishing onslaught became hauntingly vivid. With it came a slow burning resentment that he had shamelessly used her to assuage his anger against Alana.

The porch light was on, and she garaged the car before entering the house. Psychologically she was primed to do battle, although *why* was something she didn't care to pursue. It was almost as if some inner gremlin was bent on forcing an explosive confrontation, but as she switched off lights and ascended the stairs she had to concede a strange bereft disappointment in the fact that Jake had retired for the night.

Dawn brought the promise of sunshine, although the early morning frost numbed Stephanie's hands and feet as she went about her usual round of the animals. Her warm breath joined theirs, forming visible patterns in the cold air, and she moved briskly in an attempt to increase her circulation. God, it was cold! And there was still another month before the worst of winter would be upon them. It was at moments like these that she conjured up visions of warm sunshine, and she envisaged the pleasure of languishing supine on some north Queensland beach.

Chores completed, she headed back to the house, shedding her gumboots and fleecy-lined windcheater in the laundry before making for the stairs and ultimately a hot shower.

'Good morning.'

That deep drawling voice brought her to a sudden halt, and she deliberately kept her gaze lowered as she returned a perfunctory greeting.

Attired in hip-hugging levi's and a dark rib-knitted jumper that accentuated the hard muscular contours of his body, Jake emanated a raw virility that was infinitely powerful.

'I've already attended to the animals in the clinic,' he informed her, adding dryly, 'I'm about to make coffee. Will you have some?'

What did he expect? That she should ignore what happened last night and calmly share coffee with him? She shook her head slowly. 'I'll wait for breakfast.'

The sight of him at the table when she returned downstairs some fifteen minutes later gave her a shock. Somehow she had expected he would already have eaten, and the fact that he hadn't made her lips tighten with anger.

If he'd cooked something for her, she'd throw it at him! she decided vengefully. A quick circumspect inspection of the oven revealed nothing warming therein, and she set about making scrambled eggs and toast, squeezed fresh orange juice and drank it, then poured fresh coffee and carried it to the table.

Jake seemed intent on skimming the news

outlined in the newspaper, then setting it aside he poured himself more coffee.

'Enjoy yourself last night?'

She cast him a remarkably level glance, then resumed eating, giving a monosyllabic answer as she finished the last of her egg.

'Am I to be consigned to Coventry?'

It was his faintly quizzical cynicism that succeeded in bringing forth all her latent anger, and she directed him a chilling glare.

'What would you suggest—polite conversation?'

One eyebrow rose in sardonic mockery. 'Like all women upon imagining themselves wronged, you'll settle for nothing less than an apology.'

Her eyes clouded slightly with remembered pain, then cleared as she met and held his gaze. 'I'd rather have no apology at all than one that isn't sincerely given,' she said quietly, and of its own volition her chin lifted fractionally. 'And I don't imagine myself wronged—just misused as an unwilling substitute.' Rising to her feet, she tucked in her chair, and her eyes were remarkably steady. 'If you'll excuse me?'

Stephanie expected him to make some comment or at least attempt to detain her, but he did neither, and as she left the house and made her way towards the clinic her victory suddenly seemed very hollow. It was impossible to imagine any woman having the last word where Jake Stanton was concerned—much less someone with her lack of sophistication.

The clinic was busy, and apart from a hastily snatched lunch break there was little opportunity to do other than attend to the numerous animals and their owners.

It was well after five before they were able to close

up the clinic, and Stephanie was about to follow
Michael out the door when Jake called her back.

Slowly she turned, her expression polite as she
waited for him to speak.

'I instructed Mrs Anderson not to prepare
dinner,' he told her. 'We'll go out for a change.'

'We?'

He gave an imperceptible shrug, and a slight
smile tugged the edges of his mouth. 'Call it an act
of atonement, if you like.'

'I don't think so, thank you,' she refused quietly.

'I've already booked a table.'

Her gaze became level, and she even managed a
faint smile. 'I'm sure you won't have to eat alone,
Jake. There's any number of women who'll jump
at the chance should you care to lift the phone.'

A faint speculative gleam darkened his eyes.
'I've extended the invitation to you.'

'And I've refused.' She didn't add that she was
sorry, because she wasn't. 'Goodnight.'

Fool, she thought silently as she entered the
house. You could have gone out with him, a tiny
voice taunted, taken the evening with both hands
and accepted whatever he wanted to give. It could
even be fun, a chance to get to know him better as
a man, rather than as your father's locum.

Almost of its own volition, her head moved
from side to side in silent negation. There was
nothing to be gained, except heartache. A slight
bubble of hysterical laughter rose in her throat.
One had only to see Alana to know his taste in
women. How could she compete with that? Why
should she even try? Yet to deny she was unaware
of his particular brand of magnetism would be
hypocritical.

Slowly she mounted the stairs, and in her room

she stripped off her uniform and donned a casual pantsuit in emerald green velvet. It was warm, and suitable for what she had planned for the evening—viewing television, she thought with a wry grimace.

The kitchen seemed unusually cold, with no welcoming warmth or the aroma of appetising food permeating the air. A quick glance in the refrigerator revealed some leftovers, and without further ado she set about assembling herself an edible meal.

She had almost finished when she heard Jake leave the house, and perversely she felt inexplicably cross, part of her wishing he had at least ascertained if she'd changed her mind. Not that she had, she assured herself fiercely. It would have given her the greatest satisfaction to have refused again.

The house seemed empty and lonely, and nothing on television grabbed her interest sufficiently, so after fruitlessly switching channels she finally turned it off and went upstairs to her room, settling into bed with a book which she determinedly read until ten.

Surprisingly she slept, and woke to the insistent peal of the alarm next morning, aware that nothing had disturbed her through the night, not even the sound of Jake returning.

Dressed, she made her way downstairs to the laundry, where she shrugged her arms into the heavy sheepskin-lined coat before thrusting her feet into gumboots in preparation for her usual round of the animals.

Chores completed, she went into the kitchen and came to an abrupt halt at the sight of Jake sitting at the table, a mug of steaming black coffee within hands' reach.

CHAPTER FIVE

'GOOD morning.' Stephanie kept her greeting noncommittal, and saw him wince.

'Do you have to speak so loudly?'

Her gaze flew to his face, and a faint smile curved her lips at his slightly dissipated air. 'My, oh my,' she murmured drolly. 'Are you nursing a hangover?'

'A giant-sized headache,' Jake corrected wryly, shooting her a sharp frowning glance, and she grinned.

'Cause and effect—it's all the same thing.'

'Don't sound so self-righteous,' he told her. 'It's partly your fault.'

'How like a man to lay the blame anywhere but at his own feet!' she remarked, moving towards the refrigerator. 'Eggs, steak, sausages. What will it be this morning?'

'You're really getting a kick out of this, aren't you?'

She had a difficult time veiling the devilish gleam lightening her eyes. 'Why should you imagine that?'

He leaned back in his chair and regarded her with ill-concealed mockery. 'Oh, I think you'd enjoy taking me down a peg or two, Stephanie Matheson.'

'Do you want your eggs scrambled or fried?'

'Do you know I was invaded before I was halfway through the first course?' he drawled sardonically. 'A woman vowing I'd saved her darling pooch from a fate worse than death sailed

84

up to my table and sat down. Only a polite hint
that I was expecting someone to join me succeeded
in making her leave.'

'Tough,' Stephanie observed unsympathetically.

'You should have been there.'

'To keep the predators at bay?'

His eyes hardened slightly, belying the slight
smile curving the edge of his mouth. 'One day
some man is going to take you to task.'

'A few have tried without success,' she responded
with unaccustomed flippancy. 'More coffee?'

He held out the mug and she refilled it. The
meal was almost ready, and she was about to serve
it on to plates when the phone rang.

Stephanie answered, then after listening for a
few seconds she held out the receiver. 'It's for you.'

'An emergency call?'

'I really do hope so,' she declared sweetly. He'd
find out soon enough who was on the other end of
the phone, and a few seconds later Jake said
hardily,

'I thought I told you not to call me.'

Poor Alana, she thought with a twinge of
remorse. It must be hell to love with such a degree
of intensity that it removed every vestige of pride.
Not wanting to infringe, she put Jake's breakfast
in the oven to keep warm, then took her plate into
the dining-room.

She was forking the last of her egg from her
plate when Jake joined her, and she studiously bit
into some toast.

'No comment?'

At his drawled query she glanced up, keeping
her gaze steady. 'What should I say?'

'Nothing at all,' he shrugged cynically, and she
gave an imperceptible shrug.

'Impossible to even imagine you need advice on how to conduct your affairs.'

One eyebrow slanted in a sardonic arc. 'Plural? What if I were to assure I prefer a solitary existence unencumbered by the female gender?'

Deliberately summoning lightly tinged mockery, she let her mouth lift into a faint smile. 'You're not serious?'

'Perhaps not,' he drawled.

'Just requiring one ex-wife to exit the scene,' she mocked, finishing the last of her coffee.

'Yes.'

'It must be the very devil to possess so much machismo,' Stephanie declared tartly.

'Is that an admission?'

'Heaven forbid!'

'So adamant.' His faint laugh brought forth a surge of latent anger.

'You're a callous brute!' she rounded on him furiously. 'The poor woman is obviously besotted with you and wants a reconciliation.'

'Ah, yes,' Jake agreed sardonically, his eyes hardening measurably. 'Will it shock you to learn that Alana loves money and everything it can buy? Far more than anything else,' he enlightened with cynical mockery. 'She left me for someone who appeared willing to place the entire universe at her feet. Tired of playing "wife", she packed and fled to the movie capital with the promise of a fat contract and a life of everlasting fun and excitement. A life,' he added wryly, 'I neither wanted nor envied. The only word I had was via her lawyers when she filed for divorce.' He pinned her motionless with his dark gaze. 'Something that can be achieved with remarkable speed in the States. They have several trite terms suitable for every occasion. Alana chose "irreconcilable differences". God knows, it seemed to fit.' He paused, then continued hardly, 'Alas, there was no instant stardom, and her new benefactor, realising she couldn't act, cast her aside and pursued another young nubile female. One must be seen to be successful,' he told her with heavy cynicism. 'Over the next few years she sought out and deliberately courted the rich and famous, gaining bit parts in films that never reached the cinema. They were viewed, of course. Alana possesses a beautiful body, and wasn't ashamed to show every inch of it. Do I need to elaborate?'

A tinge of pink coloured her cheeks, and her eyes held a stricken look.

'Poor Stephanie,' Jake mocked. 'I do believe you're shocked. Not a pretty picture, is it?' he drawled. 'The world of beautiful plastic people began to pall, and deciding her "fling", as she called it, was over, she elected to return to Canada. I'm sure you can guess the rest?'

Stephanie found her voice with difficulty. 'You didn't want her back.'

'No,' he said brusquely. 'Unfortunately, she refused to be convinced, and I decided to return to Australia.'

'And she followed you.'

'Yes.'

'You need a smokescreen.' The words were out before she was aware she'd opened her mouth.

'My dear Stephanie,' Jake murmured slowly, 'are you offering to volunteer in that capacity?'

'No, of course not.'

His eyes narrowed slightly, then assumed a speculative gleam. 'I rather think the idea is too good to be dismissed.'

'Not *me*,' she said quickly, aware of a strange lurching sensation in the region of her heart.

'You've just been overruled,' he told her with dangerous softness.

'I won't let you.'

'Would it be so terrible?'

'It's deliberately deceitful,' she began shakily, hardly daring to look at him.

'I'll make it worth your while.'

Anger reared up inside her, sparking her eyes with fury. 'How *dare* you!'

'You're prepared to do it *gratis*?' He was laughing now, silently, showing fine white teeth. 'For love?'

Stephanie picked up the nearest thing and threw it at him, watching with mesmerised fascination as he neatly fielded the mug and set it down out of reach. A slow mounting horror at her action began to have its effect, and her voice came out as a shaky whisper.

'I couldn't love you if you were the last man on earth!'

She had to get away, out of this room, and she had taken a few steps towards the door when her arm was caught in a bruising grip.

'Not so fast,' he murmured inflexibly, turning her round and stilling her impotent struggles with an ease that was galling.

'Let me go!'

'Soon.'

There was a brooding expectancy in his gaze that made her catch her breath, and she was powerless to stop the betraying pulsebeat at the edge of her throat. 'Don't—please!' Was that her voice? It sounded strange; a kind of breathless pleading supplication that was oddly at variance with her emotions.

His head lowered, descending with seeming slow motion so that when his lips touched the vulnerable hollow beneath her earlobe it was almost an anti-climax. With feather lightness he teased the sensitive cord, trailing down with infinite provocativeness until he reached the madly-beating pulse at the base of her throat, then not content, he let his mouth drift steadily up towards her mouth.

It was like drowning, slowly sinking through soft translucent waters, making her aware of a strange feeling of helplessness, and in the need to catch hold of something tangible she clutched his arms for support.

Almost of its own volition her traitorous body robbed her of the will to think, melting against him as if it recognised some magnetic elusory pull that had everything to do with the senses.

His mouth created its own erotic havoc with a practised mastery that afterwards made her burn with mortification in the knowledge that she could be made to feel so weak. Not only to *feel*, but to subside into a state of such mindlessness so as to be totally unaware of anything but the moment.

When he finally released her, she stood perfectly still, bemused, and unable to utter so much as a word.

'Hmm,' Jake drawled musingly. 'You see? It won't be so hard, after all.'

The sound of his voice, laced with the inevitable mocking cynicism, acted like a douche of cold water.

Slowly her head lifted until she met his narrowed gaze, and her eyes were remarkably clear. 'You're a very—sensual man, with a high degree of expertise,' she managed evenly, while inwardly her heart was racing with the aftermath of an emotion so tumultuous it was frightening. 'But if you think I'll fall in with your plans, willy-nilly, you're sadly mistaken.'

His smile held an edge of cruelty. 'My dear Stephanie, I don't plan on giving you any choice.'

'You can't coerce me—I won't let you!'

Sardonic amusement gave his dark eyes a devilish gleam. 'I was thinking more along the lines of gentle persuasion.'

'I see. Imagining I couldn't fail to find it anything but a pleasurable experience, I suppose,' she said heavily. 'If you want to make it appear convincing, you'll need some co-operation—and I'm not prepared to give it.'

His gaze penetrated the barriers she had erected in defence against him, and after timeless seconds she lowered her lashes and moved away from him, attempting to bring some sanity to the situation.

'It's almost time to open the clinic.' She began clearing the table, and he let her escape. A slight shiver shook her slim frame. He resembled a sleek panther about to stalk an unsuspecting prey; assuming a certain indolence that was misleading for the unwary, but leaving no doubt that he would eventually pounce.

Somehow Stephanie managed to get through the day with the minimum of effort. The morning was devoted to surgical cases, and she dealt with several incoming calls from anxious owners, took appointments, and brought a number of files up to date prior to taking an early lunch. An emergency call ensured Jake's absence for much of the afternoon, and he still hadn't returned when Michael left shortly after five. Taking a check on the animals destined to stay overnight, Stephanie took time to murmur reassuringly to the three cats and two dogs as she placed clean newspaper in each holding cage, ensured that they had fresh drinking water, then moved back to the waiting room with the intention of locking up.

It came as a shock to see a male form standing near the doorway; even more of a surprise as he turned and she recognised who it was.

'Ian! What are you doing here?'

'I wanted to see you.'

Stephanie eyed him warily, unsure of his intention. 'I don't think that's a good idea.'

'Look, Stephanie—I've lifted the phone several times to try and explain——'

'Your actions were explicit enough,' she said dryly, and he had the grace to look ashamed.

'Look, I'm sorry about that,' he began awkwardly.

'I have to lock up, and get back to the house.'

'Stephanie, please——'

'Ian, there's no point in pursuing this conversation.'

'I don't want to give you up,' he insisted stoically. 'We've been friends for a long time.'

'We were,' she corrected with soft emphasis.

'You can't mean that!'

Her gaze was particularly level. 'I do.'

'I acted on impulse,' he began desperately. 'I was angry.'

She didn't bother making any comment, and after a few minutes he looked away, a slow tide of red creeping up from his neck to cover his face.

'There's nothing I can do or say to make you change your mind?'

'No.'

'I—I've even thought of leaving home,' he burst

out. 'I've had the offer of a good flat. It would be ideal if you would share it with me.'

'Is that a proposal or a proposition?' It was cruel of her to proffer the taunt, but her conscience urged that he deserved it.

'We could give it a try,' Ian said eagerly, his smile fading as he glimpsed her refusal.

'I really must ask you to leave,' Stephanie insisted quietly, and saw his eyes narrow.

'What if I don't want to?'

'Oh, I think you'd be advised to do as the lady says,' a familiar voice drawled from behind, and she went completely still.

'How long have you been there?' Ian demanded with a trace of belligerence as he turned to face the older man.

'Long enough,' Jake declared bluntly, his gaze razor-sharp as it raked her pale features.

'I came to see Stephanie.'

'It would appear she doesn't want to see you,' Jake asserted, levering his tall frame away from the aperture. His movements appeared deliberately lazy, yet only a fool would fail to see the dangerous glint in his eyes or not recognise the anger beneath the surface of his control.

'Are you ordering me to go?'

Jake's gaze moved slowly until it settled on Stephanie, and after a measurable silence she ventured quietly,

'I think it would be best.' Her hand lifted in an unconscious movement, then fell again. She wasn't the type who revelled in arguments, or attempting to set one man against another. Even as she considered the latter, a light bubble of hysterical laughter rose in her throat. To imagine anyone but Jake emerging the victor was ludicrous!

'We have a lot to discuss,' Ian said meaningfully, totally ignoring Jake, and she shook her head.

'No.'

'I'll ring you,' he insisted doggedly.

'Please don't.'

'You can't mean that?'

'She does,' Jake intervened smoothly, taking the few steps necessary to bring him to her side. His expression assumed wry mockery as he arched an eyebrow at the younger man, 'Do I need to elaborate?'

Ian looked as if he was about to choke. 'Then it *is* true! Mother was right——'

'I won't share,' Jake told him with sardonic cynicism, and Stephanie could only stand in shocked silence as he draped an arm about her shoulders.

'You stupid little bitch!' Ian bit out, raking her from head to toe and back again. 'He'll only use you, then where will you be? Don't think I'll have you back!'

She longed to scream that it was all a farce, that she wouldn't turn to him for anything, much less consider resuming a friendship, except that Jake's fingers were exerting a warning force over her delicate bones, issuing a silent threat she didn't care to ignore.

'You've said enough, Bryant.' His voice was dangerously soft, and she shivered, hating them both equally at that moment.

'I'll go,' Ian declared vehemently, his features dark with anger. 'I just hope you know what you're letting yourself in for, that's all!'

Seconds later the door crashed shut, and Stephanie momentarily slumped with relief, then straightened as anger replaced apathy.

'You had no right——' she began, wrenching away from his grasp.

'That's a matter of opinion.'

She rounded on him in fury. 'How dare you! Sounding just like some—feudal autocrat——'

'So indignant,' he mocked musingly.

'Yes—*yes*, damn you!'

'All I intended was a little support. In your father's absence, I owe it to him to show some responsibility.'

'You have to be joking!' she gasped incredulously. 'I refuse to believe Dad asked anything of you. Edith James, maybe. But not you.'

One eyebrow slanted with wry amusement. 'Why not?' he drawled sardonically. 'I'm far better equipped to keep the wolves from the door.'

'You forgot something,' she declared sweetly. 'Who shall I summon to help me keep *you* at a distance?'

Laughter gleamed from his eyes, and his mouth took on a wry twist. 'Rest assured you have nothing to fear from me.'

No, she didn't suppose she had, she decided wearily. A little light dalliance to serve his purpose, but nothing more. He was too cynical and much too world-weary to enter into an affair—least of all with her. Oh God, what was she thinking of! Yet she could, all too easily. The knowledge was damning and in direct contrast to her moralistic beliefs. Incredible to imagine she was so strong, so in command of her own emotions, when all it took was for Jake to project sufficient charm and she was lost.

'No comment?'

Stephanie made herself meet that mocking glance, and her voice was quite steady. 'Why endorse the obvious?' She moved towards the door. 'I've checked the post-surgery animals.'

The kitchen bore the redolent tantalising aroma of a roast cooking in the oven, and she read the scrawled note Mrs Anderson had left. An apple pie cooling on the bench-top, she perceived, and only the saucepan containing freshly-cut beans to be switched on.

As soon as the beans were simmering she replaced the lid, lowered the element heat, then went upstairs to change. The house was pleasantly warm, thanks to central heating, and after taking a quick shower she pulled on tailored slacks and a jumper, ran a brush through her tumbled curls, then made her way downstairs to the kitchen.

'Fancy going out for a few hours?'

Stephanie glanced up from spooning the last mouthful of dessert from her plate, and was unable to contain her surprise. 'Why me?'

'Why not?'

She savoured the delectable tang of apple and homemade pastry, and gave every appearance of considering a reply. 'What do you have in mind?' she said at last, and heard his sardonic drawl in response.

'I'm the stranger in town. The choice is yours.'

'The movies, nightclub, the pub,' she outlined with a shrug. 'We don't run to a variety of cultural pursuits—unless you're inclined towards a local theatre production?'

'The pub sounds fine. Neither of us will need to change,' Jake declared wryly. 'I'll help with the dishes, then we'll get away.'

Stephanie stood to her feet and began stacking plates prior to clearing the table. 'If I decline, you'll probably overrule me.'

'Are we discussing the dishes?'

Oh, he was impossible! 'Both,' she declared succinctly, and could have hit him with considerable relish as he began to laugh.

Ten minutes later she was seated in the luxurious confines of the Lamborghini as it growled—there seemed no other appropriate descriptive for the engine's sustained muted roar—down the driveway. The instrument panel looked far too complex for an ordinary mortal to decipher, and after casting it an appreciative glance Stephanie simply leaned back, determined to enjoy what must surely be a superb experience in high-powered motoring.

'Did you bring the car over from Canada?'

Jake didn't take his eyes from the road. 'Genuine interest, or polite conversation?'

Stephanie drew a deep steadying breath, then said tightly, 'If you're going to resort to sarcasm every time I open my mouth you can turn this monster round and take me home.'

'I bought it in Melbourne from a friend who no longer had need of it,' he drawled. 'Does that satisfy your curiosity?'

'I'm not a gossipy busybody intent on ferreting out information!' She felt indignant, even angry, and clenched her hands in an effort to control her temper.

'Did I suggest you were?'

Stephanie declined to answer, electing to remain silent during the short time it took them to reach the centre of town.

Within seconds Jake slid the powerful vehicle into the kerb, then switched off the engine and doused the headlights.

'Are you going to sit there and sulk, or are you coming?'

Say Hello to Yesterday
Holly Weston had done it all alone.

She had raised her small son and worked her way up to features writer for a major newspaper. Still the bitterness of the the past seven years lingered.

She had been very young when she married Nick Falconer—but old enough to lose her heart completely when he left. Despite her success in her new life, her old one haunted her.

But it was over and done with—until an assignment in Greece brought her face to face with Nick, and all she was trying to forget....

Time of the Temptres:
The game must be played his way!

Rebellion against a cushioned, controlled life had landed Eve Tarrant in Africa. Now only the tough mercenary Wade O'Mara stood between her and possible death in the wild, revolution-torn jungle.

But the real danger was Wade himself—he had made Eve aware of herself as a woman.

"I saved your neck, so you feel you owe me something," Wade said. "But you don't owe me a thing, Eve. Get away from me." She knew she could make him lose his head if she tried. But tha' wouldn't solve anything....

Your Romantic Adventure Starts Here.

Born Out of Love
It had to be coincidence!

Charlotte stared at the man through a mist of confusion. It was Logan. An older Logan, of course, but unmistakably the man who had ravaged her emotions and then abandoned her all those years ago.

She ought to feel angry. She ought to feel resentful and cheated. Instead, she was apprehensive—terrified at the complications he could create.

"We are not through, Charlotte," he told her flatly. "I sometimes think we haven't even begun."

Man's World
Kate was finished with love for good.

Kate's new boss, features editor Eliot Holman, might have devas tating charms—but Kate couldn' care less, even if it was obvious that he was interested in her.

Everyone, including Eliot, thoug Kate was grieving over the loss c her husband, Toby. She kept it a carefully guarded secret just how cruelly Toby had treated her and how terrified she was of trusting men again.

But Eliot refused to leave her alone, which only served to infu ate her. He was no different from any other man... or was he?

These FOUR free Harlequin Presents novels allow you to enter the world of romance, love and desire. As a member of the Harlequin Home Subscription Plan, you can continue to experience all the moods of love. You'll be inspired by moments so real...so moving...you won't want them to end. So start your own Harlequin Presents adventure by returning the reply card below. <u>DO IT TODAY!</u>

She shot him a dark look, then reached for the doorclasp, sliding from the car with fluid grace.

The outside air was cold, the atmosphere heavy with moisture, and Stephanie shivered after the warmth of the car, slipping her arms into the sleeves of her coat and belting it firmly at her waist.

A quick sideways glance revealed that Jake had copied her actions, and she gestured to her left. 'The hotel is in the next block.'

They walked together, and she was supremely conscious of his height and breadth, the sheer animal magnetism he exuded. He was a striking man; one who drew glances from almost every female they passed, some circumspect and others openly speculative.

Inside the cosy warmth of the hotel's lounge it was even worse, and summoning a sense of humour seemed the only way to deal with the strong pang of antipathy that closed round her heart. Something she refused to acknowledge as remotely resembling jealousy. To experience that unenviable feeling one had to love, and she didn't—she *couldn't* be falling in love with him. That would be tantamount to traversing a one-way road all the way down to Hell. Yet somehow fate was pushing them together, contriving circumstances that seemed beyond their control. She'd managed to survive the past ten days. With effort she could surely manage the remaining twenty until he left.

'You're not very communicative,' drawled Jake, his eyes darkly speculative as they roved her expressive features.

'I didn't realise you required scintillating conversation,' she essayed with a slight smile, then had to mask her surprise as he leant out a hand and trailed his fingers down her cheek.

'Are you real, Stephanie?' he mocked, the edges of his lips lifting slightly to form a slow teasing smile.

'What you see is what you get,' she quipped, faltering as she glimpsed the brooding cynicism evident.

'A pretty little girl as cute as Mom's apple pie,' he murmured, subjecting her to a deliberate analytical appraisal. 'Giving every appearance of being well-mannered, nice, and definitely the sort one takes home to meet the family.'

'You sound almost resentful,' Stephanie managed evenly, inwardly hating him. If he wanted to be a perfect brute, he was more than halfway there.

'Perhaps I am,' he said deliberately.

With the utmost care she finished her drink, then stood to her feet. 'I'll get a taxi home.'

'No.' For so softly a spoken word, it held terrible menace. 'You'll stay until I'm ready to take you.'

'I'd like to know why you brought me,' she said unsteadily, sinking down into her chair.

'Jake *darling*—you came!'

For one horrible moment Stephanie thought she was hearing things, then she slowly turned to discover that the apparition in human form belonged to none other than Alana Stanton. Jake, to give him credit, didn't move so much as a muscle to register surprise—or any other emotion, for that matter, she thought grimly. It seemed too much of a coincidence not to be contrived, and the anger welled up inside her, threatening to explode with the realisation she had been used as a pawn by a master player. It wasn't a feeling she enjoyed, and it took every ounce of restraint not to get up and walk out.

'I don't recall making an arrangement to meet you,' Jake drawled, his features deliberately expressionless, and Alana made a teasing moue.

'But darling, you knew I was staying in town.'

'Did I?'

'I told you—on the phone, when I rang this morning.'

'You're wasting your time—and mine.'

'I can't believe that.' Eyes welled with tears and she clutched hold of his shoulder. 'Jake, please—don't do this to me!'

With calm deliberate movements he removed her scarlet-tipped fingers.

'I love you!' Alana whispered, distraught, and Stephanie thought she would die at the cold remoteness in his eyes.

'You're incapable of giving that emotion to anyone but yourself.'

'Oh, Jake, how can you say that?'

Stephanie couldn't stand it any longer, and glancing from one to the other she rose to her feet. 'If you'll excuse me?'

Jake's eyes narrowed thoughtfully, and for one crazy moment she thought he meant to detain her.

'The ladies' room,' she elaborated, daring him to say so much as a word.

'I'll keep him amused while you're gone,' Alana husked, her eyes hungrily searching his face. She didn't even bother to glance in Stephanie's direction, and offering a tightlipped smile Stephanie moved towards the foyer.

From there she stepped quickly through the main entrance and turned towards the taxi-rank, seeing with a sinking heart that there were none in sight.

Damn! She couldn't afford to wait too long in case Jake elected to investigate her absence. Inevitably there would be a scene, but at the moment she was too consumed with anger to care.

Five minutes passed, and still the rank remained empty. With a heavy sigh she determined there was nothing else for it but to begin walking. Four kilometres wasn't too great a distance, and besides, she needed the cool sharp air to help clear her senses and the exercise would do wonders in working off a vast amount of inner rage.

She set out briskly, glad of the sensible shoes she had chosen to wear, even more thankful she hadn't changed into a dress. At least in trousers, a thick jumper beneath her coat, she was well protected against the elements.

A few cars sped past, and she quickened her step as the risks involved suddenly penetrated. The road was hardly isolated, being the main thoroughfare in a westerly direction from town, and there were houses—although as she gradually left the township itself they grew sparser. There was no real cause for concern, she assured herself mentally, beginning to wish she hadn't acted so rashly.

It began to rain, a soft dampening drizzle which soon became whipped by a steadily driving wind, and she cursed afresh, thrusting her hands deep into the capacious pockets of her coat. Within minutes it was raining in earnest, soaking through her trousers until they became sodden, and water trickled down her nape to find its way beneath the turned-up collar of her coat.

The illuminating glow of approaching headlights precipitated her to move off the road on to the bordering gravel, giving the car plenty of room to pass, and her stomach gave a sickening lurch as she heard it slow down, then come to a halt abreast of her.

A quick sideways glance was sufficient to identify the gleaming silver metal, and for one crazy moment she didn't know whether to be apprehensive or grateful.

The driver's door slammed, and scant seconds later hard hands bruised her arms, then without any more ado she was hauled bodily sideways and thrust into the car's interior.

'Make one move to get out, and I'll thrash you within an inch of your life!' Jake growled the instant before he slammed the passenger door, then he crossed round and slid in behind the wheel to send the car forward with a burst of speed.

'The water from my clothes will damage your upholstery,' Stephanie said through chattering teeth. She was so cold she began to shake with it, and all the anger and abuse she longed to hurl at him remained unsaid. An unbidden voice taunted any attempt in her present state would be nothing short of ludicrous!

His choice of epithets was explosive. 'To hell with the upholstery,' he snapped savagely, sparing her a rapid scrutiny. What he saw made him swear, and she closed her eyes against such suppressed violence, willing the powerful car to transport them home as quickly as possible.

It did, and in no time at all she was being bundled indoors like a recalcitrant waif, much to her indignation.

'Do you have to be so—brutally *bossy*?' she flung resentfully, hating his easy strength, the sheer masculinity he exuded.

'Get those wet clothes off,' Jake instructed in a tone that was nothing less than a command, and she cast him an angry glare.

'I fully intend to,' she returned waspishly, peeling off her drenched coat. Her hands shook, and with an impatient gesture he helped her tug her arms free. 'I can manage,' she bit out, hating him afresh.

His eyes raked her mercilessly. 'You stupid little fool,' he grated harshly. 'You'll be lucky if you get away with just a cold—let alone anything else. Now get upstairs and into a hot bath. I'll fix you a stiff brandy.'

'I won't drink it, I hate the stuff.'

A menacing glint leapt into his dark eyes. 'If you don't do as you're told *now*, I'll make myself responsible for ensuring that you do.'

'You wouldn't dare!'

'Try me.'

Capitulation was obviously the only course she could take. The consequences of defying him didn't bear thinking about, she decided shakily as she turned and made her way upstairs. He was too much—too arrogant, too self-assured, and far too ruggedly handsome for his own good.

Upstairs she went into the bathroom and turned on the shower, then dispensed with her clothes. She was soaked to the skin and each individual garment clung, making it difficult to undress.

The hot needlespray was a welcome relief, and she shampooed her hair, luxuriating in the steamy warmth as her limbs slowly lost their frozen numbness, gradually returning to life, and after an age she reluctantly closed the taps. A large fluffy towel took care of the excess moisture from her body, and, dry, she wrapped it round her hair and donned her pyjamas and dressing-gown. It was too late to bother putting on clothes, she decided wryly as she plugged in her electric hair dryer.

Within minutes the wet straggly length of her hair was restored to dry curling softness, and she surveyed her features in the mirror, deciding that she looked none the worse for her ordeal—if one could call a two-kilometre walk in pouring rain an ordeal.

Her discarded clothes lay in a sodden heap in the bathtub, and she elected to leave them there until morning. The thought of squeezing them out and carrying them downstairs to the laundry didn't appeal. At the moment all she wanted to do was fall into bed.

Crossing the hall to her room, she came to an abrupt halt at the sight of Jake standing lazily at ease just inside the doorway.

'What are you doing here?'

He lifted the tumbler he held in his hand. 'To ensure you drink this.'

Her eyes met his with a touch of defiance. 'I told you I didn't want anything. If you remember, the last time I drank some it made me ill.'

A muscle tensed along his jaw. 'That was because you were foolish enough to take tablets at the same time.'

She moved forward, stepping round him in order to reach her dressing-table where she picked up a brush and tugged it through her hair, then she turned to face him. 'If you'll kindly leave? I want to get into bed.'

His gaze was remarkably level. 'Trust me, Stephanie, and drink it, hmm?'

That was the living end. 'Trust you?' Her eyes

flashed with opalescent blue fire. 'Why the hell should I?' Her breasts heaved with the force of her pent-up anger. 'Everything you do has an ulterior motive. Not only have you deliberately suggested there's something between us in an attempt to shake off your wife—your *ex*-wife's attentions—as if that wasn't bad enough, tonight you arranged to see her and dragged me along as an unwilling and totally ignorant decoy!' A sudden bout of the shivers shook her slight frame, followed by a horrendous trio of sneezes which she found difficult to cope with and still project the right degree of indignant anger.

'In the name of heaven—get into bed!' Jake growled emotively, and when she made no move to obey him he placed the glass down on a near-by pedestal.

'What are you doing?' Stephanie demanded, her eyes widening as he came towards her, and she took a backwards step as he reached for the ties that belted her dressing-gown. Firm fingers quickly dispensed with the knot before she had a chance to desist, and in a battle of force there could be only one victor.

'As I thought,' he drawled with a slight smile. 'Pretty pink, but hardly the latest fashion in alluring nightwear.'

'What did you expect?' she retaliated with swift fury. 'Sheer nylon and lace?'

He gave a deep sigh that behoved great patience. 'Will you get in beneath those covers, or must I put you there?'

'You damned well would, wouldn't you?' she retorted resentfully, giving in with obvious reluctance. The bed was deliciously warm, and she realised he must have switched on the electric blanket while she was beneath the shower.

'Now, the brandy,' Jake insisted, reaching for the glass.

'And if I refuse, I suppose you'll hold my nose and pour it down my throat.' It wasn't a question, merely a statement of intent which he admitted with damning urbanity. 'I think I hate you,' she muttered hollowly. 'In fact, I'm sure I do.'

'Don't let it bother you,' Jake said smoothly, holding the glass to her mouth.

Stephanie cast him a venomous glare the instant the raw spirit hit her lips. Undiluted and warm, the liquid stung in her throat, then slid smoothly down to her stomach. One sip was enough, and she pursed her lips against any more.

'Be a good girl, hmn?' he coaxed, but when she remained resolute he drawled softly, 'I intend staying here until you drink it, even if it takes all night.'

'So I have to choose between the lesser of two evils,' she flipped incautiously, and saw his eyes narrow and darken.

'You're hardly in a position to bargain.' His voice was inflexible and vaguely menacing, almost as if he had come to the end of his tether.

'Oh, for heaven's sake,' she muttered wretchedly, reaching for the glass. 'I'm in no mood for male domination.' Her fingers came into contact with his, and she retreated as if from an electrical charge. 'Give me the glass, damn you, and I'll drink the blasted stuff.'

'You won't fling the contents in my face, or worse, tip them on to the floor?' he taunted, retaining the glass firmly against her lips.

With that she simply leant slightly forward and took the liquid in one long swallow without thought to its effect. 'Satisfied?' she demanded trenchantly, hating him anew. 'Now, get the hell out of my bedroom!'

Satan, who had been lolling head between paws just inside the door, became instantly alert, his head high, ears pricked at the slight note of hysteria in his mistress's voice.

'I didn't intend to stay,' Jake told her with veiled mockery, and she missed the clinical assessment in his gaze as he stood upright and moved away from the bed.

Stephanie closed her eyes, then tried and failed to summon any further resentment. She seemed to be slowly floating towards merciful oblivion, deliciously warm both inside and out. Tomorrow, she decided drowsily, would be time enough for recriminations—right at this moment she didn't care to be bothered with anything.

CHAPTER SIX

THERE was a note propped up against her bedside clock, making it the first thing she saw when she opened her eyes next morning.

Stay where you are. Have taken care of 'home' animals. Mrs Anderson will bring you breakfast in bed.

Indignation replaced curiosity as Stephanie read the vibrant scrawl, and it was only as she replaced the note on to the pedestal that she became fully aware of a series of aches and pains racking her recumbent form. Even her arm seemed strangely heavy as she slid it back beneath the bedcovers.

Stay in bed, indeed! she thought resentfully. How could she? As if she would, anyway!

The way she was feeling was doubtlessly related to the quantity of brandy she had had last night. A wry grimace twisted her lips as she reached for the covers and tossed them aside. This terrible weightiness of limb and brain had to be a hangover. Inevitably she would feel better on her feet—better even when she'd eaten.

After the initial few minutes she had to concede the former to be incorrect, for even dressed and having completed her toilette she experienced no improvement, and if anything felt worse. Her head seemed to be filled with cottonwool, slowing the motor responses from her brain, so that every movement she made appeared to be in slow motion.

A sudden shiver made her seek an additional

cardigan to put on over her uniform, then she made her way downstairs to find Mrs Anderson putting the finishing touches to a breakfast tray in the kitchen.

'My dear, I was about to bring this up to you.'

Quite clearly the good lady was astonished, and Stephanie cursed Jake afresh.

'As you can see, I'm fine,' she began lightly, meeting the older woman's gaze with equanimity.

'You look rather pale. Are you sure you feel all right?'

'A bit headachey, but nothing a few Paracetamol won't cure.' She sat down at the table and summoned enthusiasm for the appetising meal placed before her. Normally she would have done justice to the plate of steaming porridge, toast and coffee, whereas now she could only manage a few token mouthfuls before replacing the spoon. The coffee quenched her thirst, and she refilled the cup and drank it before realising that it was almost nine-thirty and she was an hour late for the clinic.

Quickly she rose to her feet and left the house, going into the waiting room seconds later to find Michael attending to reception, three canine patients awaiting attention, and no sign of Jake.

'What brings you here?' Michael quizzed almost beneath his breath. 'I was told you were ill in bed.'

'Well, I'm not,' she disclaimed shortly, pulling the appointment book towards her. 'Are these files in order?'

'They are. I've just made a two o'clock appointment for the Goodsons' Benji—routine shots.' He frowned slightly, then suddenly grinned. 'Oh yes, our favourite and most regular pooch Bartholomew is being presented for inspection at ten.' He shot her a swift encompassing glance. 'Are you sure you're okay?'

'Such concern over a tiny head cold,' she mocked, pulling the portable typewriter towards her and rolling paper through the platen. 'If I didn't know better, I'd think you were trying to make me feel redundant.'

'I'm going,' murmured Mike, sloping her a cheeky grin, and she was saved from further comment by the insistent peal of the telephone.

Somehow she managed to get through the day, although by the end of it she was hardly able to speak and she felt as if she was burning up with a fever.

Jake, upon casting her a brief hard glance when he became aware of her presence in the clinic, held back whatever he had in mind by way of remonstrance until late afternoon when the last patient exited with its owner.

'Get the hell out of here,' he said tersely, then speared Michael with a brooding glare. 'Get on to an agency and find a replacement receptionist for what remains of the week, and tentatively part of next.'

'You can't do that,' Stephanie protested, then to her total chagrin fell into a coughing spasm that left her far more weakened than she imagined possible.

'I just did,' he asserted with unnecessary force. 'One more word out of you and I'll have your hide, understand?'

Michael's expression was comical, then assumed shrewd speculation as he glanced swiftly from one to the other before crossing to the desk.

'After you've made that call,' Jake instructed brusquely, 'make another to her doctor. Request a house-call, but if that's not possible, tell the receptionist I'll bring her to the surgery now.' He cast her a brief encompassing appraisal. 'If necessary, I'll speak with him myself.'

'Hey, who do you think you are, giving orders as if I have no say in the matter?' she spluttered indignantly.

'You don't,' Jake returned succinctly, and she glared at him, aware of Michael's voice in the background as he spoke on the phone.

'You're nothing but a damnable tyrant,' she choked, trying to inject a degree of vehemence into her voice and failing miserably. Her vocal chords seemed to have lost all their former power, and attempting forceful speech only resulted in a mortifying whisper that totally lacked conviction.

The only response she received was a wry scrutiny that served to incense her further, and she longed to hurl something at his hatefully arrogant head!

'All dealt with,' Michael announced with satisfaction. 'Doctor Reynolds has another call to make in the area, and should be here around six-thirty. The agency have a number of temporary receptionists on their books, and guarantee one of their girls will report for work tomorrow morning.'

So much for imagining she was indispensable!

'I'll push off,' Michael continued, glancing at Jake for verification. 'Unless you want me to stay?'

'No,' Jake said briefly, and when the younger man had left he let his glance skim over Stephanie's slim form. 'For God's sake go home and get into bed. And don't,' he warned softly, 'so much as open your mouth to refuse.'

She longed to give vent to her anger, but she didn't possess the energy to do anything but temporarily concede defeat.

Once inside the house she made her way wearily upstairs, collected clean pyjamas and took a leisurely shower, then turned back the covers and slid into bed.

She must have dozed off, for it seemed only minutes later when Jake walked into her room, and she merely glared at him.

'Soup,' he indicated, placing the tray down on to the pedestal. 'Sit up and have it. The doctor should be here soon.'

She tried to voice a scathing retort, but no sound emerged from her lips, and she could only direct him a baleful look.

He, damn him, simply stood there and waited until she'd spooned the last drop, then took the tray and left.

Dr Reynolds arrived shortly afterwards, conducted a thorough examination, added a homily on the inadvisability of walking without adequate protection in the cold winter's rain, then filled two pages of his prescription pad.

'I'll hand these to Mr Stanton to have filled,' he declared, standing to his feet, then replacing everything back into his bag, he snapped it shut, then spared her a kindly look from beneath drawn grey brows. 'Plenty of fluids, take all your medication, and for the next few days, stay where you are.'

Stephanie wanted to be indignant, to say she only needed a good night's rest, and with the aid of antibiotics could easily return to work—if not tomorrow, then the day after. Except that a dreadful lethargy seemed to have taken control, making her feel totally enervated, and she simply sank back against the pillows and closed her eyes.

A hand shaking her shoulder forced a reluctant response, and she let her eyelids sweep slowly upwards. She wanted to tell whoever it was to go away and leave her alone, except that her tormentor was flagrantly persistent, insisting on wakefulness as she was bodily lifted into a sitting position.

Jake's face swam into view within the incandescent glow projected by the bedside lamp, and she wasn't capable of offering resistance as he pressed a succession of tablets, one by one, into her mouth aided by an alternating sip of water.

Events over the next twenty-four hours retained a haziness in which some things penetrated and others remained beyond recollection. She remembered someone changing fever-soaked pyjamas for fresh ones, being bundled into blankets while sheets were renewed, and it seemed fluids were being forced between her lips with too frequent regularity.

When next she woke it was night, and although she felt weak, the listless weightiness of her limbs had gone. The strange woolliness in her head seemed to have disappeared too, and feeling dreadfully thirsty she reached out a hand to switch on the bedside lamp.

There was a pitcher of diluted fruit juice as well as water, and she took a glass and carefully poured in some juice. Its taste was sharp and refreshing, satisfactorily slaking her thirst, and she was about halfway through sipping the contents when she let her eyes rove slowly round the room.

All of a sudden she froze, unable to comprehend for an instant that the spare bed just five feet distant was occupied. Not only that, she discovered with mounting consternation, but the dark watchful gaze observing her every move belonged to none other than Jake himself.

'What are you doing here?' The words slipped out unbidden, and she watched with mesmerised fascination as he levered his powerful frame into a sitting position. His chest was bare, and the thought rose hysterically to mind that he probably wore little else but briefs beneath the covers.

'You've regained your voice.'

Surprise registered momentarily, to be quickly replaced by a surge of indignant anger. 'Why are you sleeping in my room?'

'Purely out of necessity,' he drawled. 'I can hardly keep an eye on you from the other end of the house, and suffering temporary laryngitis there was no way I would have been able to hear you.'

'Why should you want to?'

His mouth sloped to form a wry smile. 'My dear Stephanie,' he informed her tolerantly, 'you've been in the grip of a raging fever for the past two days. If you hadn't come out of it by morning, the good Doctor Reynolds was going to put you in hospital. We've all been most concerned.'

'Good heavens!' Her eyes widened with the knowledge, then clouded as patches of memory rose to the surface. 'You played nursemaid.' It was a statement that needed no verification, and a delicate pink crept into her cheeks. She wanted to declare aloud that she couldn't see him in that role, but the words remained unsaid. Jake Stanton was capable of anything, and answerable to no one for any of his actions. She supposed she should be grateful. 'Thank you.'

'So politely spoken,' he acknowledged with an

edge of mockery. 'If there's nothing you want or need, I suggest you switch off the light and go back to sleep. In case you hadn't noticed, it's the middle of the night.'

A need to use the bathroom surfaced, and while there Stephanie washed her face and cleaned her teeth.

Back in her room she surveyed his prone form and the words tumbled out without much coherence. 'I'm all right now. There's no need for you to stay.'

'Pretend I'm not here, there's a good girl, hmm?'

'I insist you leave,' she said shakily, her eyes becoming large in a face pale from the aftermath of her illness. 'Please.'

'I don't sleepwalk,' Jake drawled gently. 'And your virtue was never in safer hands.'

'That might be,' she conceded hollowly, slipping into bed, but just knowing he was there would preclude relaxation. As for sleep—impossible! 'Please, Jake.' Even to her own ears, her voice seemed cracked with distress, and to her utter chagrin her eyes filled with tears.

His husky oath was barely audible, but nonetheless harsh. 'Stephanie—for the love of heaven, stop it!' He slipped back the covers and reached for his robe at the bottom of the bed, shrugged it on, then stood to his feet and belted the ties.

In two strides he was looming over her, tall and infinitely forbidding, and she didn't seem capable of uttering so much as a word.

'I'll sleep in the room next to this one,' he declared hardily. 'With both doors left open.'

She could only nod, her eyes wide and luminous, and with a strangely gentle movement he leant forward and brushed his lips against her forehead.

'Barely warm,' he murmured, giving a slight smile. 'I believe the worst is over.'

Stephanie didn't say a word. For some strange reason she wanted to lift her arms and link them together behind his neck, then draw his head down to hers. There was an elemental danger in harbouring such thoughts, yet even as she attempted to dismiss them his mouth slid down, closing each eyelid in turn, then she felt his lips trace a dangerously evocative path as they erased her tears.

She wanted to protest, but the will to offer any resistance deserted her, and as his mouth closed over hers she simply parted her lips as if to do so was the most natural thing in the world.

It could have been mere seconds, or several minutes later that Jake lifted his head and placed a finger gently to her lips.

'Now off to sleep, hmm? I'll see you in the morning.'

Stephanie watched as he left the room, feeling a deep longing ache somewhere in the pit of her stomach. It was madness, she decided shakily—an illusion brought on by her obviously weakened state, a combination of medication and the witching midnight hour. To imagine anything else demanded more than she could mentally cope with, and feeling suddenly tired she leant out and switched off the lamp, plunging the room into darkness.

Over the following few days Stephanie showed a steady improvement, and was permitted downstairs for the first time on Sunday.

Mrs Anderson had prepared sufficient soup to last the entire weekend, as well as several appetising dishes with which to tempt Stephanie's palate. As for Jake, he had proved a watchful if faintly aloof guardian, insisting upon limiting her physical exertions to an essential few, supervising the food she ate and the amount of rest he considered desirable to her convalescence.

No mention had been made in connection with the circumstances surrounding her flight from the hotel lounge, although as her strength returned so did a measure of resentment. With time on her hands she began to brood, her mind becoming increasingly active with thoughts of the enigmatic man who had become so much a part of her life. Two weeks seemed an age, yet what could she possibly hope to achieve in so short a time? And there was Alana. Jake might not want her, but there could be little doubt his beautiful ex-wife wanted *him*.

Jim Matheson had written once, and phoned twice in the space of the past week, and it was obvious from his exuberance that the lecture tour was a huge success. By tacit agreement with Jake, Stephanie refrained from mentioning her lapse in health and was able to reassure him that the clinic was running smoothly with no unforeseen problems.

Sunday afternoon was a typical midwinter's day, the cold air whipped by a fierce wind that howled round the corners of the stone house and whistled against the eaves and chimneypots. Every now and then rain lashed against the windowpanes in intermittent showers.

From her curled-up position on one of the capacious recliner chairs in the lounge Stephanie cast the outside elements a rueful glance, then scanned the television programme for something inspiring to view.

The phone rang, and she was about to answer it when the sound was cut off mid-peal. Jake, she concluded, had picked it up from the study.

Karen had visited yesterday, spending most of the afternoon, and various other friends had rung during the past few days. Only Ian had maintained silence, and for that she was grateful. Strange that they now appeared to have so little in common—if in fact they ever had, she pursued sombrely. It chilled her to think the young man she thought he was, the essential character, didn't really exist, which surely proved just how superficial their friendship had been. Two weeks ago, if anyone had suggested Ian could behave in such a fashion, she would have laughed and dismissed it as ridiculous.

'I have to go out to the Robertsons' farm,' Jake declared from the doorway. 'Their prize heifer is showing all the symptoms of a difficult calving.' He lifted a hand and thrust it through his hair, ruffling it into attractive disarray. 'I'll get back when I can.'

Attired in faded levi's with a dark blue vee-necked sweater stretched over broad shoulders, he looked ruggedly attractive and his appearance set up a familiar increase in her pulse-beat, making her unusually cross.

'At least you can get out of the house,' she declared with a trace of petulance.

'If that little barb is meant to evoke sympathy— forget it.'

Indignation rose to the fore. 'I don't want your sympathy!'

'I declare you're almost back to normal,' he drawled.

'If you mean I'm tired of being cossetted, you're darn right. In fact,' she declared, 'I'm coming back to the clinic tomorrow.'

'You're not,' Jake told her unequivocably. 'Thursday is the soonest I'll consider it.'

'*Thursday!*' she choked in disbelief. 'You have to be joking!'

'Not at all.' He moved into the room and came to stand in front of her.

'If you say one word about how ill I've been, I'll——'

'What?' he queried imperturbably, amusement lurking in the depths of his eyes.

'*Scream,*' she snapped furiously, and he laughed.

'Poor Stephanie,' he mocked, leaning down towards her. 'Mrs Anderson has left every imaginable delicacy prepared to tempt your appetite. There are enough books and magazines available to satisfy the most dedicated reader. A sophisticated electronic recording system and a veritable library of taped cassettes.' His shoulders lifted in an indolent shrug. 'Music, television. What more do you want to keep you amused?'

She could have hit him, in fact she seriously considered it, except she wasn't sure she could cope with the consequences. So she settled for simply glaring at him instead.

He watched each and every fleeting emotion as it mirrored itself in her eyes, then a husky chuckle sounded deep in his throat as he bent low and bestowed a lingering kiss to her softly parted lips.

'You'll catch my cold,' Stephanie murmured in protest, and he straightened, his dark eyes agleam with devilish humour.

'Then you can take a turn at playing nurse-maid.'

She felt her eyes widen fractionally, then she masked their expression. 'You wouldn't let me.'

'Would you want to?'

Unsure whether he was serious, or simply baiting her, she responded lightly, 'Men make terrible patients—doctors worst of all. I'm quite sure a vet would be totally unmanageable.'

'Me, especially, eh?'

She tilted her head, proffering him a sweet smile. 'I'm sure of it. I'd request Dr Reynolds to pre-scribe vast quantities of medicine, then personally ensure you swallowed every drop.'

'And when I'd recovered sufficiently to re-taliate?'

Even imagining him in bed brought forth a latent longing she was powerless to suppress. 'I'd love to pursue this conversation—really,' she assured him with seeming solemnity. 'However, I don't think Mr Robertson will appreciate a stillborn calf, do you?'

His sloping grin did strange things to her equilibrium, and she watched as he turned and left the room. Within seconds she heard the front door close, then the powerful roar of the Land Rover as it reversed out from the garage and sped down the driveway.

It was five hours before he returned, and Stephanie had already eaten. She heard him enter the house and go straight upstairs to shower and change, and by the time he came into the kitchen she had his meal on the table.

One glance at the weary set of his shoulders was enough to tell her that all had not gone well. 'Shall I get you a drink?'

Jake gave a wry grimace as he slid out a chair and sat down. 'I need one, but now not. I may have to go out again.'

'That bad?' she queried, and received a faint smile.

'A prolonged birth, but mother and one calf are fine. The same can't be said for its twin. The next few hours are crucial, and Robertson will phone if there's a change for the worse.'

Stephanie eyed him keenly. 'What's your opinion?'

He picked up cutlery and began eating. 'A fifty-fifty chance of survival.'

At that moment the phone rang, and she sped to answer it offering a fervent prayer it wouldn't be Mr Robertson with bad news. On hearing Alana's seductively husky voice she said simply, 'Yes, he's here,' then held out the receiver.

Jake took it from her, and within seconds his features hardened.

Wanting to be anywhere else but in the position of eavesdropper, Stephanie stepped past him with the intention of leaving the room and came to an abrupt halt as a hand closed over her arm. Her eyes flew to his, her surprise evident at his action, and she almost died at the degree of pitiless resolve tightening his expression.

'In the name of heaven, Alana,' he declared hardly, 'get the hell off my back, otherwise I'll be forced to have a restraining order placed on you!'

The receiver was slammed down with considerable force, and Stephanie winced.

'If you don't loosen your grip, I'm likely to be nursing a broken arm!'

She rubbed the offended limb as he returned to the table and resumed eating. He offered no apology or explanation, and with a mental shrug she turned back to extract a portion of apricot crumble that had been warming in the oven. There was whipped cream to go with it, and she crossed to the refrigerator to extract the small bowl.

Jake had just spooned the last of his dessert when the phone rang again.

'I'll get it,' he said tersely, rising to his feet, and after a few curt directives into the receiver he replaced it. 'Robertson. It's as I feared, I'm afraid. I'll have to go out.'

Stephanie merely nodded, knowing his mind was preoccupied, and as he strode from the room she began clearing the table.

An hour later just as she was on the point of going upstairs to bed the headlights of a vehicle swept an illuminating arc through the glass panel beside the front door, chasing the shadows in a rapidly changing pattern as it drew steadily closer.

Expecting the lights to swerve into the garage, she experienced a mixture of curiosity and concern when they stopped right outside the main entrance, then were doused, and within seconds a knock sounded on the front door.

Exerting caution, she slipped the security chain in place before answering, and there was no way she could hide the shock of seeing Alana standing there.

'May I come in?'

Damn, Stephanie cursed inwardly. What should she do? 'It's rather late for a social call,' she began tentatively. 'In any case, Jake isn't here.'

'He shouldn't be long, surely?' the glamorous redhead said with a winsome smile. 'I'll wait until he comes back.'

At that moment the powerful lights of the Land

Rover came into view, and Stephanie breathed a sigh of relief. Jake was infinitely more capable of dealing with his errant ex-wife than she could ever be. Quite frankly, the ultra-sophisticated Alana deflated her composure, making her feel inadequate and very young. Perhaps, she conceded wryly, by comparison she was—in terms of worldly experience, Alana was light years ahead.

The Land Rover pulled into the garage, and less than a minute later Jake's tall frame loomed into view. It was impossible for him not to recognise Alana, but if he was surprised he gave no sign. His expression was an enigmatic mask, yet Stephanie glimpsed the tired lines spreading from the corners of his eyes, the imperceptible weary set of his shoulders.

In seeming slow motion she watched him enter the foyer, followed closely by Alana, and as he turned towards her she lifted her hand in an impotent gesture, then murmured something inane and totally irrelevant. They resembled three players on a stage, about to be manipulated by a master script, except that she had no knowledge of the lines. The silence seemed to grow and echo, until in desperation she invented an excuse to escape.

'Don't go, darling,' Jake began silkily, and with two lithe strides he moved to stand at her side, his smile so infinitely warm and intimate it was all she could do not to reel back with shock, and she stood immobilised as his arm curved over her shoulders. 'I think now is as good a time as any to announce our plans, don't you?'

'Plans?' Alana queried delicately, her finely pencilled brows narrowing slightly, and it was no small feat that Stephanie managed not to echo that monosyllabic query.

'Marriage.'

She didn't know who was more surprised. Her mouth opened, then closed, rather like a gasping fish, she decided with a touch of hysteria.

'If this is your idea of a joke, I'm not amused!' Alana snapped, her eyes becoming glittery with anger.

'You should know me well enough to realise I wouldn't joke about making such a serious commitment,' Jake drawled, his eyes narrowing as Alana shifted her gaze towards Stephanie and subjected her to a swift raking scrutiny—rather like a superior feline assessing and dismissing an insignificant fieldmouse, Stephanie decided wildly.

'You can't be serious?'

Stephanie could hardly blame Alana for voicing incredulity. She herself was stunned into virtual speechlessness!

'Do you doubt me?' Jake drawled with all the deadly softness of a preying jungle beast. He had to pounce—it was all part of the game.

'You can only have known her a matter of weeks,' Alana began, and he corrected smoothly,

'Two, to be precise—almost to the day.'

Alana's brows rose, slightly arching in calculated disbelief. 'Hardly long enough, would you say, darling?'

He regarded her solemnly for what seemed an age, then he ventured quietly, 'Stephanie has all the qualities a man most admires in a woman.'

Alana's expression became shrewdly speculative. 'Oh yes,' she acceded with apparent kindness, although no one could doubt the thinly-veiled mockery evident. 'And such a help, being a vet's daughter. I never was much good at anything vaguely to do with domesticity, was I, darling?' she purred, sending him a blatant glance from beneath her long thick-fringed lashes. 'But then you always seemed to prefer me in the bedroom to anywhere else.'

'I admit you could, to put it bluntly, turn a pretty trick,' Jake drawled, his eyes hooded, and Stephanie made an instinctive movement to escape which was instantly stilled. 'However, physical lust eventually palls when unaccompanied by fidelity.'

'Noble, if a mite outmoded,' Alana remarked with a slight provocative smile. 'These are the eighties, darling.'

'We should never have married. An affair would have been infinitely more preferable,' he opined with sardonic cynicism, and the woman laughed.

'Oh, come, we had a good year or two, surely? I can remember a time when you were totally besotted.'

'It isn't possible to relive the past, Alana,' he said mockingly. His arm tightened on Stephanie's shoulders, then he leaned down and brushed his lips against her temple. 'I've found the girl with whom I'd like to spend the rest of my life.'

If she just stood perfectly still, kept her eyes lowered, and could contain her rapidly rising anger, surely this—this *charade* would eventually come to an end, Stephanie decided blindly.

Some of her inner tension must have transmitted itself, for he trailed his lips down to her mouth and covered it with his own, then he lifted his head and gave Alana a sardonic smile. 'I'm sure it must be painfully obvious that your presence is superfluous?'

'I'll go,' Alana said tightly, her eyes alive with bitter enmity. 'But don't imagine you've heard the last of me.'

Jake's expression hardened into a cruel mask. 'Should I take that as a threat?' he demanded silkily, and Alana looked as if she was ready to strike him.

'I don't like losing.'

'How can you lose something you never really had?'

The ensuing silence was such that Stephanie was almost afraid to breathe, and she watched in mesmerised fascination as Alana turned and swept towards the door. Seconds later it slammed with resounding force, and was closely followed by an engine revving powerfully to life, then the car was driven away at breakneck speed to pause with a squeal of brakes as Alana negotiated the turn at the end of the long driveway.

With considerable care Stephanie extricated herself from his grasp and slowly turned to face him. Steeling herself to be calm, she lifted her chin and met his enigmatic gaze. 'Perhaps you'd care to explain?'

He regarded her in silence for what seemed an age, then he lifted a hand to his hair to rake his fingers through its thickness before letting his arm fall to his side. 'Damn it, I'd reached the end of my tether!' he vented with an emotive growl.

'My God,' Stephanie breathed, 'you've got a hell of a nerve, dragging me into it!' All the pent-up rage she'd managed to suppress bubbled up inside her as the words tumbled out in a furious flow. 'Damn you! I won't be used as a convenient scapegoat!'

'I've tried everything I can think of in an attempt to convince my charming ex-wife that a reconciliation is out of the question,' Jake said brusquely, his eyes flint-hard and implacable.

'And I just happened to be handy in your scheme of things,' she opined wrathfully. 'Tell me, do you always ride roughshod over everyone?'

The look he cast her was ruthlessly formidable. 'Only when it's absolutely necessary.'

She drew in a deep breath and expelled it slowly. 'I sincerely hope your ex-wife keeps the so-called "news" to herself, otherwise the town gossips will have a field-day.'

'With luck, she'll return to Melbourne and board a plane for the States within the next few days.'

Stephanie gave a sigh that behoved great forbearance. 'Dare I remind you of the quotation— "Heav'n has no rage, like love to hatred turn'd, Nor Hell a fury, like a woman scorn'd"?' Rather wearily she lifted a hand to her throbbing temple. 'I'm going up to bed. Goodnight.' Without looking at him she moved to the stairs, and was halfway up them when he drawled,

'Make sure you take your tablets. I wouldn't want to incur Mrs Anderson's wrath should you suffer a relapse.'

She didn't bother responding, nor did she deign to spare him a glance. In fact, it was just as well there was considerable distance between them, otherwise she would surely have *struck* him!

CHAPTER SEVEN

STEPHANIE slept badly, and woke the next morning feeling decidedly fragile. Perhaps it was pique that persuaded her to remain in bed rather than face Jake over the breakfast table, although she preferred to think of it as an act of self-indulgence. Being a convalescent gave her licence to do as she pleased, and she elected to take full advantage of it—for today, at least.

She should have known it wouldn't work, she thought resignedly as shortly after eight o'clock a sharp double knock on her door was immediately followed by Jake's entry into the room.

'Don't you ever wait to be asked?' Stephanie thrust waspishly as she pulled the covers up to her chin and held them tightly in place.

He, darn him, looked incredibly *vital* dressed in hip-hugging trousers and a vee-necked aran-knit jumper. His dark eyes subjected her to a rapid assessing glance before returning to rest on her stormy features.

'My dear Stephanie,' he drawled, 'would you willingly invite me into your bedroom?'

She tossed him a venomous glare and refused to rise to the bait.

With easy lithe strides he crossed to stand within touching distance, and his expression bore compelling intentness.

'Okay, let's have it, shall we?' he began imperturbably.

'Is this an act of childish perversity, or are you

genuinely feeling unwell?'

'Both,' she snapped, daring him to pursue it further.

Without a word he caught hold of her hand and took note of her pulse, then let his fingers trail over her forehead. 'A slightly elevated pulse, but no temperature.'

'I'm not an animal!' she retorted indignantly, and was further enraged by his husky laugh.

'Oh, I don't know,' he allowed musingly. 'At the moment you resemble a skittish kitten—claws unsheathed and full of spitting fury.'

'Go away, Jake.' If he didn't she was liable to say something regrettable.

'I'll leave a note for Mrs Anderson to bring you something to eat,' he declared imperturbably, and she flung back instantly,

'Don't bother. I'm getting up.' An idea occurred to her, and she voiced it without thought. 'In fact, I think I'll drive into town and spend a few hours shopping.'

'The hell you will,' he responded succinctly. 'It's about two degrees outside, and raining heavily.'

'Then I'll come into the clinic—if only for a while,' Stephanie insisted.

'Tomorrow,' he allowed reluctantly, and she shook her head in defiance.

'This afternoon. I'm tired of being cooped up like an invalid!'

'Tomorrow,' Jake insisted silkily. 'I'll arrange for Maryanne to have the afternoon off.'

Her eyes narrowed faintly, and she frowned as a niggling suspicion fought its way to the fore. 'Maryanne *who*?' There were only two local girls who bore that name, and one in particular was a striking brunette with a personality to match.

'Sylvester,' he divulged. 'Michael is definitely enamoured.'

'And you, of course, are not,' she declared with seeming sweetness.

'My, my,' Jake murmured quizzically. 'If I didn't know better, I'd almost suspect you were jealous!'

That did it. Without thought she lunged out at him, missing her target as he sidestepped with ease, and she tumbled to the floor in an ignominious heap trailing the top sheet which had somehow managed to get caught up on her foot, plus part of the blankets and the coverlet.

His deep husky chuckle only added insult to injury, and she picked up the nearest object and threw it at him.

The slipper was fielded and tossed to the floor, and she watched in mesmerised fascination as his eyes hardened with deliberate intent, his movements studied as he slowly bent down towards her.

Even as she scrambled to escape, his hands closed over her arms, lifting her clear of the tangle of bedclothes, and she struggled as he set her down before him.

'Let me go, damn you!' He was dangerously close, his stance vaguely menacing, and she was suddenly conscious of her attire, the fact that her pyjama top had parted at the waist, and one button had come adrift from her exertions. With shaking fingers she attempted to pull the edges of the top together, and couldn't because his hand was already there, the warmth of his fingers creating havoc as they slid to cover her breast.

'Don't!' It was a useless plea that went unheeded as he lowered his head and trailed his lips down the sensitive cord of her neck to the rapidly-beating pulse at the edge of her throat.

Not content, his lips slid further, and she uttered a silent moan as they closed over one roseate peak, teasing it gently until it became a sensitised pulsing ache that sent shivers of ecstasy spiralling from the very core of her being.

She was aware of his hands closing over her waist, pulling her close, then they moved slowly up her back holding her fast as his mouth slid up to close over hers in a kiss that made anything she had previously experienced pale into insignificance.

The earth moved, she was sure of it—certainly she became mindless, lost and locked in a passionate arousal that knew no bounds. All that was important was that he didn't stop, and she clung to him unashamedly.

Then suddenly she was free, and she could only look at him dazedly, her lips pink and faintly swollen as they parted in mute protest. At that precise moment she felt as if she had suffered the loss of a limb, so acute was her desolation.

His muttered imprecation brought colour to her cheeks, and a return to sanity, as slowly she came down from the sensual plateau to the full realisation of what she had almost allowed to happen.

'I think you'd better leave.' Was that her voice? It sounded low and husky, an almost inaudible murmur that whispered shakily into the stillness of the room, and she was powerless to stop the tears that began to well with shimmering brilliance in her eyes.

A muscle tensed along his jaw and his eyes darkened until they resembled obsidian chips, then with an abrupt movement he turned and left the room.

Slowly she sank down on to the edge of the bed and buried her face in her hands. What on earth was happening? Up until now she had thought she could remain in full control of her emotions, but what had just transpired proved how easy it was to succumb to the moment.

How long she remained there she had no idea, and it was only when she heard the faint sounds of Mrs Anderson's arrival that she stirred, forcing her limbs to move as she stood to her feet. Like an automaton she remade her bed and tidied the room, then she collected fresh underwear and made for the bathroom.

A leisurely shower did much to restore her composure, and dressed, she caught up a warm sheepskin-lined coat, slipped her feet into knee-length boots, then went downstairs.

In the kitchen she poured herself some coffee and made some toast, exchanged pleasantries with Mrs Anderson, then despite that good woman's reservation about the advisability of going out, she collected her bag and took her leave.

Regardless of being idle for almost a week, the Datsun sprang to life and didn't falter as Stephanie backed it out from the garage, and seconds later she sent it purring down the driveway.

There were a number of cars lining the main street, and she parked without difficulty. With no clear indication of how to fill in the ensuing few hours she decided on a reasonably brisk walk along the main street. That at least would be beneficial after the past week's inactivity. There was a nice coffee lounge where she could indulge in a capuccino, and there was no reason why she shouldn't embark on a shopping spree.

Three hours later she unlocked her car and deposited a number of variously assorted carry-bags on to the rear seat, feeling satisfied with her purchases. In fact, the entire morning had been a very pleasant experience. There was nothing to compare with a successful shopping expedition to give a very necessary boost to one's morale!

The fact that her arrival home happened to coincide with Jake's lunch break hardly daunted her at all. He could be as disapproving as he liked, she thought vengefully. It was her home, she was over twenty-one, and he had no jurisdiction whatsoever where she was concerned.

Stephanie took her purchases upstairs and placed the packages on the spare bed, then removed her boots in favour of warm slippers, hung up her coat, and after casting her mirrored reflection a cursory glance she turned and left the room.

Jake was already halfway through his meal when she joined him at the table, and she offered a slight smile, determined to project an air of normality.

'Enjoy yourself?'

Stephanie continued helping herself to some excellent stew, then replaced the ladle and picked up her fork. 'Immensely,' she assured him, summoning enthusiasm. 'It was good to get out.'

'Despite being told not to go,' he slanted silkily, and she returned his gaze with equanimity.

'I didn't realise your word was law,' she responded evenly.

'Where you're concerned, it is.'

'Oh?' Her surprise was feigned. 'You're not my jailor. I'm free to do whatever I please.' Resolve gave her the courage to add, 'What's more, I'm coming to the clinic this afternoon.'

'Maryanne is extremely capable. You'll be superfluous.'

I just bet she is, Stephanie thought darkly. 'I'm sure I can find something to do,' she shrugged with seeming carelessness.

'Afraid you're not as indispensable as you imagined?' Jake queried sardonically, and it took considerable effort to remain calm.

'No one is indispensable,' she proffered sweetly, then added softly, 'Not even you.'

If she wanted to make him angry, she didn't succeed.

'Your father rang while you were out,' he told her, and her dismay was evident. 'I was able to reassure him that you're fit and well, and that everything is running smoothly.'

'What else did he say?'

'Simply that he's enjoying himself, and finding the lectures very informative.'

'Nothing else?'

'He sent you his love.'

Stephanie felt her eyes mist with sudden tears. She missed her father, his friendly tolerance and calm unflappable manner, which combined with a quizzical sense of humour made him a very dear man.

'There's more,' Jake continued with a cynicism that made her look at him in silent query. His expression bore a watchful scrutiny underlined with a certain hardness. 'Your father's call wasn't the only one I received this morning. It seems my charming ex-wife has been busy. A reporter from the local newspaper rang to confirm that information given them was accurate, and if so, they would like to run an article on how local vet's daughter has been caught up in a whirlwind romance with locum; engagement announcement, photos—the usual thing,' he concluded mockingly.

'You're joking!' Her incredulity was genuine, and her eyes widened as he shook his head.

'Unfortunately not.'

Her fork remained poised in mid-air, her meal forgotten. 'Obviously Alana decided to call your bluff.'

The edges of his mouth curved to form a wry smile. 'Obviously.'

'So,' Stephanie began carefully, 'she'll soon discover the truth.'

His gaze was remarkably direct. 'No.'

Her eyes swept over his features with mounting disbelief. 'What do you mean—*no*?'

'The reporter is due here late this afternoon, together with a photographer.'

'Look,' she began earnestly, 'it was bad enough when it was a relatively simple deception. If the media get hold of it, the whole town will know.' Her eyes darkened with pain. 'How will it look when you leave?' A surge of anger rose to the surface. 'Or perhaps I should have guessed,' she said bitterly. 'You've already taken that into consideration. Tell me, who is going to jilt who?'

'I don't like this any more than you do,' Jake intimated brusquely, and she flashed back,

'But I'm expendable. A convenient "nobody" who'll do in the circumstances. Never mind that I live here, and will have to face a veritable barrage of questions afterwards. That, of course,' she said with considerable sarcasm, 'is incidental to the lies I'll have to tell. What about my father? Have you given a thought to him?' Her eyes blazed with fury. 'Or am I supposed to take him into my confidence and explain that it was all a worthless pretence?'

'You're overreacting.'

'The hell I am!' She replaced her fork with care. The desire to throw it down, or preferably, at the hatefully calm countenance of the man seated opposite was a temptation almost too difficult to resist. With unhurried movements she stood to her feet. 'I should never have let you implicate me in the first place. But it stops here, *now*.'

Jake viewed her with an indolence that only served to increase her resolve. 'Sit down, Stephanie,' he commanded softly. 'I'm not all through yet.'

'Well, *I* am!'

'At least listen to my proposition before you discount its possibilities.'

'There's nothing you can say that will make any sense out of this,' she returned heatedly.

'Sit down, there's a good girl,' he said placatingly, ignoring her venomous glare.

'Oh,' she hissed, 'don't patronise me! I'm not a naïve teenager prepared to fall in with your slightest whim for the promise of a smile and a furtive kiss or two.'

'Furtive?' he drawled. 'I had the distinct impression that each particular occasion was entirely spontaneous—and mutually enjoyable.'

There had been several times over the past two weeks when she had been convinced she hated him, but none compared with now. 'Did I give that impression?' The desire for revenge was paramount, and she took it without hesitation. 'You do possess a certain machismo,' she offered sweetly, tilting her head to view him with detached appraisal. 'Your physique is passable, I suppose, if you like an abundance of sinew and muscle.' Her gaze didn't falter. 'As a lover, one can only imagine you're adequate.' She summoned a careless shrug. 'Quite frankly, you don't turn me on at all.'

A deep rumbling laugh rose from his throat, and the dark speculative gleam in his eyes made her blush.

'Are you throwing down the gauntlet, Stephanie?'

'Don't be ridiculous,' she choked. 'You'd be the last man I'd want to know——'

'In the biblical sense?' Jake slanted quizzically, and with the minimum of movement he reached out and caught hold of her hand. 'Don't run away just yet. We need to discuss how we're going to handle this afternoon's session with the local reporter.'

Any attempt to wrench her hand from his grasp only met with dismal failure, and short of resorting to a struggle she had little option but to remain where she was.

'What do you have in mind? A tête-à-tête where we sit holding hands and project a tissue of lies as to how we've both fallen wildly in love?' She felt close to screaming with pent-up rage. 'Even if I could bring myself to say the words, my expression would portray instant denial. The thought of gazing at you adoringly makes me sick!'

'Oh, I think you could manage it,' Jake murmured mockingly. 'You can pretend to be overwhelmingly shy, rest your head into the curve of my shoulder, and leave all the talking to me.'

'No!'

'When it's time for me to leave,' he continued as if she hadn't spoken, 'we'll let everyone assume I'm busy locating a new practice, after which you'll visit Melbourne, supposedly to check out the accommodation I've bought, arrange the redecoration, that sort of thing. A week or two later you return home,' he drawled cynically, 'minus engagement ring, and so very thankful you've found out in time what a lucky escape you've had.' He gave a lazy shrug. 'I'm quite prepared to be the villain of the piece. You can attack me with suitable malediction to convince everyone you had just cause.' His eyes narrowed thoughtfully. 'As compensation, you get to keep the ring, your so-called sojourn in Melbourne will involve an all-expenses-paid holiday, and I'll escort you wherever you want to go; theatres, nightclubs—whatever you choose.'

'You think everything has a price, don't you?' she derided bitterly.

'Doesn't it?'

'I think what angers me more than anything else is the fact that you expect me to comply,' Stephanie managed quietly, stung by his acerbic tone.

'Yet if I ask, you'd refuse,' he mocked. 'It's easier this way.'

'You're forgetting something,' she returned with matching mockery. 'I've already refused.'

'You'll look foolish if you back out now,' he pointed out silkily. 'It's gone too far.'

'And you imagine that gives you licence to——'

'Take your name in vain?'

'*Yes*—damn you!'

Ignoring her, he slid back his sleeve-cuff and gave a slight grimace as he glimpsed the time. 'I'm due back at the clinic. I'll have Maryanne ring through to the house when the reporter arrives.' He was already on his feet, his movements unhurried as he pushed in his chair.

'You're taking a hell of a risk,' she threw angrily. 'I could easily deny the whole thing in front of him.'

Jake slanted her a wry glance. 'If you were going to deny it you would have done so last night.' His lips curved to form a cynical smile. 'Relax, Stephanie. It really won't hurt at all.'

That's what you think, she felt like screaming out at him. I hurt all over, and it gets worse every day. I don't want to be involved with anything that brings me close to you—anything that will fracture the tenuous hold I have on my emotions.

As he turned and walked towards the door it took considerable effort not to hurl something at his departing back!

With a gesture of impatience she pushed her plate to one side, her appetite gone. The thought of spending the afternoon alone was infinitely depressing, and with determined resolve she cleared the table, told Mrs Anderson she would be at the clinic for most of the afternoon, then gathered up her coat.

A week's absence had wrought little change, although it rankled considerably to see Maryanne sitting behind the reception desk coping with such admirable ease.

'Stephanie, should you be back so soon?' Brown eyes widened with a show of concern. 'Jake said I could have tomorrow afternoon off so that you can get slowly back into the swing of things, but I didn't imagine you would come in today.'

So it was *Jake*, was it? A hollow laugh died in her throat. What else did she expect? Jake wasn't the formal type, and Maryanne was anything but backward in taking her chances where she could!

'I feel fine,' she said lightly, giving a faint smile.

'Just experiencing the classic symptoms of an almost recuperated patient—boredom.' She gave a slight shrug. 'I thought I'd look in and see how you were coping, and maybe help with the files or answer the phone for an hour or two.'

The other girl cast her a speculative glance beneath thick mascara-fringed lashes. 'Well, everything is up to date. Michael mentioned something about making up accounts ready to send out at the end of the week. Do you want to start on those?'

Maryanne had certainly settled in well—almost too well, Stephanie thought wryly. 'Good idea.' She moved behind the desk, pulled out a chair and sat down, then reached for the appointment book.

The phone rang, and she automatically moved to answer it, only to find Maryanne had picked up the receiver. The girl's manner was smoothly professional, yet pleasant, and Stephanie tried to dampen down a vague feeling of irritation. This was her domain, and she wondered why it bothered her to have anyone usurp it. Honesty forced her to admit that if her temporary replacement had been comfortably middle-aged, she wouldn't even give it a thought.

'Hey, welcome back.'

Stephanie glanced up and met Michael's warm grin, and reward him with one of her own.

'You look pale and thin,' he perceived. 'And I doubt you should even be here.'

'Thanks,' she responded wryly. 'Just what I need to give my confidence a boost!'

'Seriously, we've all been concerned about you. Why risk a relapse?'

'My thought entirely,' a deep voice drawled, and she glanced beyond his shoulder to see Jake regarding her with a dark inscrutable expression.

'Anyone would think I'd been close to death's door!' she parried with an attempt at humour.

Jake leaned forward and picked up a file. 'Simpkins' Bridget is next?' His glance rested on Maryanne, his eyes faintly enquiring.

'Mrs Simpkins rang to say she'd be delayed,' the girl responded. 'I was about to bring the following file forward.' She handed it to him with a vivacious smile. 'Fortunately Mr Bradburn and Sheik arrived early.'

The magnificent German Shepherd was worthy of his name, and one of Stephanie's favourite patients. As he drew close he paused at his master's heels and lifted his head so that she could lean forward and fondle his ears.

'You re-scheduled those two appointments I mentioned?' Jake asked, and received Maryanne's affirmative.

At three o'clock Stephanie made coffee and set out some biscuits. Jake and Michael would have theirs in between patients, and neither appeared to place any importance on its tepidity, or otherwise.

By three-thirty the waiting room was empty, and Stephanie was about to question why when the door opened and a man and a woman walked in. Their reason for being there was obvious, and she cursed herself for not remembering. No, that wasn't strictly true. It was something she'd put at the back of her mind in the hope that it would stay there. Now it surfaced with a vengeance.

The local newspaper, journalist and photo-grapher, the interview they planned with Jake's permission—and supposedly hers.

'The house, I think,' Jake indicated with an urbanity Stephanie resented, and, mindful of both Maryanne and Michael's curiosity, she simply followed his lead. Not difficult as he caught hold of her hand in a grip that made it impossible for her to break free.

'Go with the flow', a tiny voice prompted inside her brain. Well, it sure as hell was the only way she was going to get through however long it took for the journalist to complete her interview.

The photographer clicked away with apparent delight as Jake alternatively curved Stephanie close against him, and smiled tenderly into her eyes. All the time he offered information, answered questions, then when it all seemed too much, he very smoothly called a halt.

Afterwards Stephanie could only admire his adroit professionalism, and she watched in a daze as they left, Jake showing them out and following them towards the clinic. Tomorrow it would be news, and she didn't care to contemplate the consequences.

CHAPTER EIGHT

THOSE next few days were something Stephanie never wanted to relive again.

From early Tuesday morning the phone rang with repeated persistence, and she accepted the expressed congratulations with suitable aplomb, agreeing with a slightly hysterical attempt at humour that indeed she had been swept off her feet. A lot of the calls were genuine, but unfortunately there were a few that were not.

One from Ian fell into the latter category, and she had just finished telling him what she thought of him when she received a call from Mrs Bryant. That too was hardly a pleasant experience.

Michael managed a mournful façade for all of an hour in an attempt to let her know he regarded her misplaced affections to be a defection of sorts, then he gave one of his inimitable grins and declared he was delighted.

Maryanne looked piqued, but managed to overcome it whenever Jake emerged into the reception area.

As for Mrs Anderson, she seemed overwhelmed by this latest turn of events, and vowed she'd seen it coming for days. Stephanie, and least of all Jake, didn't care to disillusion her.

There was also the matter of an engagement ring. At Jake's insistence they drove to Melbourne Wednesday afternoon, and in one of the city's exclusive jewellery stores he requested that a number of quality rings be brought out for inspection.

Stephanie was almost afraid to choose, and after she had deliberated for several minutes the manager, no doubt recognising a potential client of obvious means, excused himself on the pretext of retrieving a few items from the safe.

'I don't want one at all,' she whispered fervently, and met Jake's sardonic amusement.

'It's essential window-dressing,' he murmured, and she retaliated fiercely,

'So I have to grin and bear it!'

'Something like that.'

In the end it was Jake's selection that graced her slender finger. A magnificent diamond set in platinum and mounted on a slim gold band, it looked far too valuable to wear, and Stephanie said as much as they walked from the store.

'It suits you,' he said with a careless shrug, and nothing she said succeeded in changing his mind.

Friday morning over breakfast he dropped a verbal bombshell. At least, it certainly felt like one.

'I'm taking you to meet my parents.' Just like that, with all the calmness of announcing a drive into town.

'I beg your pardon?' Stephanie swallowed a mouthful of coffee, then carefully replaced her mug down on to the table.

'Appropriate, don't you think? They're expecting us for the weekend.'

'You're joking! At least, I hope you are,' she added quickly.

'I'd like to leave as soon as the clinic closes,' Jake drawled, rising to his full height and negligently pushing in his chair. 'Make sure you pack something adequate for dining out. And suitable attire for Flemington. They're keen racegoers.'

'I could take my entire wardrobe,' she offered with a flash of temper, and he reached out and tapped her nose.

'Don't be facetious.'

'Are you going to allow me the afternoon off to make myself beautiful? At a guess, I'm meant to impress.'

'Why not the whole day?' Jake slanted, his eyes creasing with cynical amusement.

'Thanks,' she said wryly. 'I needed that.'

'You'll do fine as you are.'

'You mean—no expensive session with the beautician? I'm disappointed.'

His expression was impossible to discern, but his voice held laughter. 'I'm due at the clinic.'

'How typical,' she sneered, shooting him a dark glance. 'Just for that, I will take the afternoon off.'

'Maryanne will be there.'

'In that case, why am I worrying?' she managed sweetly, and could have hit him for the low husky chuckle he gave as he left the room.

'Is this really necessary?' Stephanie demanded, standing in the hall with her overnight bag at her feet. She wasn't at all sure a weekend spent in Jake's company was wise. Even worse, spending it with his parents and having to maintain an affectionate front.

'It's my weekend off,' Jake reminded her smoothly. 'What more natural than to take my new fiancée home to meet my parents?' His dark glance skimmed over her slight frame, then settled with brooding appraisal on her finely-etched features. 'Besides, it will do you good to get away.'

'Great,' she retorted with a trace of truculence. 'At least the effects of turning my life upside down haven't escaped you.'

His eyes became faintly hooded. 'I was thinking more in terms of your health.'

'My goodness, don't tell me you want to make amends?'

He reached out and trailed his fingers down her cheek, then tilted her chin. 'Don't be sarcastic.' He gave a half-smile, and she endeavoured to resist its melting effect. 'My mother will love you,' he promised softly.

'Hooray,' she mocked, sending him a wry glance. 'After the flak I've been receiving the past few days, any warmth will be a welcome change.'

'Hmm,' he drawled. 'Perhaps I should do something about that.'

As his hands settled on her waist she pulled backed in alarm. 'Don't,' she said involuntarily, her eyes widening as his head lowered down to hers.

'Shut up,' Jake murmured gently scant seconds before his lips began a teasing evocative trail over the delicate bones of her face.

His touch sent the blood pulsing through her veins like quicksilver, making her bones fluid and infinitely malleable so that she swayed towards him, her body traitorous and totally at odds with the dictates of her brain.

Of their own volition her hands wound slowly up to clasp themselves behind his head, and there was no power on earth to stop the way her mouth parted beneath his, inviting its possession like a flower to the morning sun.

His slow sensual exploration did strange things to her equilibrium, and she was barely conscious of the inaudible moan that rose in her throat, a silent plea for him to go on without thought to where it might lead. The slow ache that had begun in the region of her stomach increased until it became an agonising pain demanding release—the release only his body could give, and the knowledge had an alarming effect, stilling her response as she tried to pull free.

'What's wrong?' Jake demanded huskily, and she could only look at him, seeing the deep slumbrous passion evident in those dark eyes so close to her own.

'This is,' Stephanie whispered shakily, and felt rather than saw his slight smile.

'What could be wrong about something that feels so right?'

His faint cynicism acted like a douche of cold water. 'You don't give a damn, do you?'

'Because I react like any red-blooded male with a warm giving woman in my arms?' There was tension evident, and with it a certain hardness that made her want to cry.

'Go to hell, Jake,' she condemned hollowly.

'I've trodden that path—all the way there, and back. I don't aim to repeat the experience.'

'Then leave me alone!' Her voice was raw with painful emotion, and his gaze narrowed.

'Don't get involved, Stephanie,' he warned. 'I can't promise I'll live up to your expectations.'

'Involved!' she exploded. '*Expectations!* What do you take me for? A naïve love-struck fool? My God, you must possess a giant-size ego!' Her eyes flashed with barely controlled anger. 'I know exactly what you are, Jake Stanton. An analytical calculating bastard who'll use anyone to further his own ends!'

'Have you finished?'

'Yes!' she fairly screamed at him, hating herself for resorting to childish temper.

'Then let's go.'

'I'm not going anywhere with you!'

'You are,' he declared pitilessly. 'Even if I have to pick you up and carry you.'

'Try it!'

He regarded her silently for timeless seconds, taking in her stormy features, the defiance, then without a word he lifted her over one shoulder, bent to collect the straps of both overnight bags into one hand, and opened the front door with the other.

'Put me down, you—you fiend!' Stephanie hissed as with careless agility he hooked a foot round the door and brought it closed behind him. It was just as well it was dark. Heaven knew what anyone witnessing the scene would think, she considered, struggling wildly as he moved towards the car.

With an ease that was galling he unlocked the passenger door and tossed in their bags, then placed her recalcitrant form on to the seat and leaned over to fasten the safety-belt.

Even as she tried to undo it, he smiled, and in the projected light from the small interior pilot, it had a chilling effect.

'Escape is impossible,' he told her ruthlessly. 'I've engaged the door's self-locking device.' With that he slammed the door, and she watched him stride round to slip in behind the wheel.

'I hate you!' It was said with deadly vehemence, and earned a wry slanting glance.

'At the moment, I imagine you do.' The engine sprang to life from a deft twist of his wrist, then purred as he sent the vehicle down the driveway with swift competence.

They reached the outskirts of Melbourne in a

relatively short space of time. Stephanie kept her attention steadfastly on the passing scenery, the delicate tracery of street lights as they stretched into the distance, and listened to the tape Jake had inserted into the cassette-deck, likening the forceful tones of various classical masters to the man himself.

The intensity of her dislike was such that it precluded any thoughts as to his parents, the weekend ahead, and it was only when the powerful Lamborghini had negotiated the inner city and was heading in an easterly direction that she identified with her surroundings.

Kew was a gracious suburb, its homes providing a pleasant blend of old and new by vying with modern town houses and apartment blocks. It was into the underground car park of one of the latter that Jake eased the vehicle, bringing it to a halt in a numbered space alongside a superior Rolls-Royce.

A key-operated elevator took them high to a penthouse suite, and within seconds an intricately-carved door was flung open to reveal an elegantly attired woman whose features were alive with pleasure.

'Jake, it's so good to see you!' She gave him an affectionate hug, then stood back a pace to regard Stephanie with uncontrived warmth. 'Stephanie. You're every bit as beautiful as Jake described you. Do come in.'

Beautiful? She sent Jake a quick glance, then offered his mother a faint smile. 'It's very kind of you to invite me.'

'Nonsense, my dear. We're delighted to have you.'

Now that she was actually here, the enormity of what she was undertaking began to have its effect.

Jake's hand pressed into her waist, to all intents an outward gesture of devoted attention, but his fingers held a steely strength as if daring her to misbehave.

'Dinner will be in half an hour,' Mrs Stanton declared, leading the way into a luxuriously furnished lounge. 'Bart is on the phone—it rang only seconds before you came—but he'll join us in a few minutes, then we'll have a drink and get to know one another better.' She glanced up at her son. 'I've put you both in the guest wing.'

'I'll get rid of these,' Jake indicated the bags, and his mother gave an approving nod.

'Do that, darling. When you come back you can pour us a drink.' As if to set Stephanie's mind at rest, she explained, 'We enjoy a constant flow of visiting relatives and friends. The guest wing is quite private, and has spectacular views. I'm sure you'll like it.'

Whatever happened to old-fashioned convention? Stephanie contemplated with abstracted confusion as Mrs Stanton's implication sank in. God forbid she should share a room with Jake, let alone a bed! The thought was enough to send her into a state of near hysteria which Jake's return to the lounge did little to lessen.

Perhaps it was as well that Bart Stanton entered the room simultaneously with his son, and the ensuing introduction coupled with an adroit flow of conversation and the bolstering effect of very good sherry provided a necessary diversion.

Dinner was served at eight and comprised four courses, each a superb complement to a very well planned whole, and Stephanie's compliment was genuine, even if she failed to do complete justice to the meal.

'My dear, don't feel you must apologise,' Rebecca Stanton dismissed kindly. 'Jake has already told us you've been ill, and I've no doubt your appetite will return before long.'

She was so nice, it was almost more than Stephanie could bear, and in Bart Stanton she saw exactly the man Jake would be in thirty years' time. Mellowed, but still retaining an excellent physique; possessing a quiet strength that would prove invaluable to the woman in his life, and in Bart there was none of the cynicism so clearly evident in his son.

They took coffee in the lounge, and during the ensuing conversation there was no mention made of Alana, perhaps by tacit agreement, although there was no awkwardness apparent. Jake's parents obviously assumed he had told her of his previous marriage and any details he felt were relevant.

'It's after eleven,' Jake declared with seeming regret, and Stephanie looked momentarily startled, having lost track of time.

'Of course,' Rebecca said gently. 'It's important Stephanie doesn't become overtired.' In one fluid movement she rose to her feet and took Stephanie's hand in hers. 'Sleep well, my dear, and don't worry about getting up early. We rarely breakfast before eight-thirty at weekends.'

Jake moved forward and brushed his lips against Rebecca's forehead. 'I intend taking very good care of her, never fear.' As he straightened he curved an arm round Stephanie's shoulders and the look he cast her held a warm intimacy that left no doubt as to just how he intended taking care of her.

Consequently Stephanie felt a faint blush colour

her cheeks, and her proffered 'goodnight' fell as little more than a stammered whisper.

The guest wing was a stunning addition to a perfectly co-ordinated suite, comprising a lounge and a large bedroom with en suite facilities.

As soon as the door closed behind them, Stephanie turned and gave him a vitriolic glare. 'How dare you!' she whispered vehemently, and was further incensed as she glimpsed his wry smile.

'Don't accuse me of something I haven't yet done,' Jake warned softly. 'Or I may become sufficiently tempted to turn fiction into fact.'

'The bedroom has a double bed.'

He gave an indolent shrug. 'There is a second adjoining suite with twin beds, but obviously Mother thought this more appropriate.' A lazy smile curved the edges of his mouth. 'I didn't like to disillusion her.'

Stephanie had great difficulty containing her temper. 'You mean, you took great delight in keeping her in ignorance.'

'Not deliberately.' He lifted a hand and ran it through his hair, ruffling it into attractive disorder. 'How does one explain in this age of permissiveness that a newly-engaged couple supposedly on the verge of matrimony require not only separate beds, but separate rooms?' He slanted a quizzical glance that held a tinge of sardonic humour, and it only served to heighten her rage.

'You don't, by any stretch of the imagination, expect me to share this room with you?' she demanded with chilling wrath.

'The bed is large,' Jake drawled. 'Large enough for both of us with ample space to spare.'

'You have to be joking!' Incredible that she

could still speak, as the connotations envisaged almost paralysed her vocal chords! 'I'll use the sofa in the lounge.'

One eyebrow rose in cynical appraisal. 'You expect me to play the gentleman and offer you the bed?'

For a moment she almost insisted, then reason recognised that the sofa would never accommodate his lengthy frame. 'No.' She stepped past him and picked up her bag. 'I'm going to have a shower.' Not bothering to look at him, she moved towards the bathroom, and once inside carefully shut the door. There was no lock, and she tried to be philosophical about it as she showered in record quick time, then, her toilette completed, she slipped a robe over pyjamas and emerged into the bedroom.

Jake was sitting propped against the pillows, a book in hand which appeared to have his entire attention, and she felt a frisson of shock slither down the length of her spine at the sight of so much muscular bare flesh. The least he could have done in the circumstances was to don pyjamas, she thought crossly, then became even more angry as she realised it was probably a deliberate ploy on his part.

Without a word she crossed to the lounge and shut the communicating door with a sense of relief. The sofa looked comfortable, and she was about to subside into it when a silent curse escaped her lips. Central heating provided superficial warmth, but she'd need a blanket, and a pillow. That meant going back into the bedroom.

Stephanie knocked, and heard Jake's voice drawl an answer, then with a faint grimace she turned the knob and re-entered the room.

Fixing her gaze on a point somewhere above his left shoulder, she said steadily, 'I need a pillow.' She indicated the spare one resting beside him, then eyed the thrown-back coverlet. 'I'll take that as well.' Suiting words to actions, she quickly gathered them up and moved towards the door.

'Sleep tight, little girl.'

His sardonic mockery was the living end, and without thought she turned and threw the pillow at him. Even as he fielded it she saw his expression change, and one glance was sufficient to send spirals of alarm scudding in countless different directions.

'Come and get it,' Jake commanded softly, and with a strangled refusal she turned and fled.

Her heart was racing and her breathing came in ragged gasps as she reached the lounge—ridiculous, when she considered the distance. Half expecting him to follow and take some retaliatory action, she leaned against the closed door counting the seconds until she was convinced he had none in mind.

With her robe folded beneath her head and the coverlet doubled and tucked around her slight form she tried to cull sleep without success. The longer she tried the more difficult it became, and she lay staring wide-eyed into the darkness cursing Jake afresh, crediting him with every dastardly deed she could summon. It didn't aid sleep, but it sure got rid of an awful lot of pent-up frustration!

The sofa, which at first had seemed reasonably comfortable gradually took on the resemblance of a rack, its buttoned leather hard and unyielding as she endeavoured to relax, and her makeshift pillow became lumpy. What was more, the heavy coverlet seemed like a dead weight, and she gave a despairing groan. At this rate she'd get no sleep at all, and resemble a walking zombie at breakfast—which doubtless would amuse Jake in the knowledge of his parents' likely suspicion of the cause.

For the umpteenth time she stood to her feet and rearranged her bedclothes, spreading the coverlet out and folding it so she could slip in between its enveloping folds.

A sudden stream of light took her unawares, and she glanced up to see Jake framed in the aperture, his features darkly indiscernible.

'One word,' he breathed with dangerous softness as he advanced towards her, 'just *one* word out of you, and I'll beat you senseless!'

With numbed fascination she watched as he plucked the coverlet and her robe from the sofa and threw them into the bedroom, then with the minimum of movement he lifted her into his arms and strode into the adjoining room.

Without pausing he crossed to the bed and dropped her down on to it, plumped the pillow, then tossed the blanket over her shocked form.

'Make a move to get out, and I'll haul you back so fast you won't know what happened!' he thrust with pitiless disregard, crossing round to climb in beside her, adding with chilling finality, 'And if you think I have designs on your virtue, forget it. My preference runs to warm willing women aware of every facet of sensual pleasure—not untutored innocents in need of persuasion!'

The light was extinguished, and Stephanie lay shaking with mortifying rage. She longed to turn and thump him, fight with all the tenacity of an infuriated she-cat. Only the knowledge that she couldn't win prevented her, and she seethed, silently plotting his downfall, until sleep finally claimed her.

At some stage of the early morning hours she stirred, and on the periphery between sleep and wakefulness she became aware of tangled images racing just out of reach into a frightening void.

She had to be dreaming, subconsciously seeking a solace that appeared so real she could actually feel arms gathering her close and the gentle brush of lips at her temple.

A small contented sigh emerged, to be replaced almost immediately by startled comprehension as reality dawned, and she came fully awake in an instant. Rigid with shock, she pushed against him, her voice stark with fear.

'Let me go!'

Stephanie felt him move, then there was a click and the bedside lamp threw out a soft illumination.

'You were dreaming,' Jake told her wryly. 'From the way you were moaning and threshing around, I'd say it was definitely nightmarish.' His eyes narrowed as they swept her disturbed features. 'You've been crying.'

Her hands shook slightly as she brushed them across her cheeks in a hasty attempt to remove any traces of tears. She felt incredibly vulnerable, and a frightening mixture of emotions fought for supremacy as a strange weakness invaded her limbs.

'Want to talk about it?'

'I don't even remember what it was about,' she faltered, finding his close proximity unbearable. For some reason she wanted to reach out and touch him, let her mouth linger against his skin, and as for the rest of it—her eyes momentarily

closed in self-defence against what he might read
in their depths. Like a wild insatiable hunger the
demand for fulfilment rose within, almost devour-
ing her, and she forced herself to turn away from
him, deliberately controlling her breathing. 'Please
switch off the light,' she managed quietly, closing
her eyes, and she unconsciously tensed as she felt
him move, then the room was plunged into
darkness.

When she woke it was daylight, and Jake stood
fully clothed beside the bed holding a cup and
saucer.

'Come on, sleepyhead, it's well after eight.'

'Why didn't you wake me?' She struggled into a
sitting position and took the cup from his hand.
The coffee was black, hot and sweet, just the way
she liked it, and she sipped appreciatively.

'My parents have planned for us to attend the
races at Flemington with them. I agreed we'd go.'
His expression held a lazy warmth. 'Do you mind?'

'Of course not. I love horses.' It was true. Their
movements were poetry in motion, although given
a choice she far preferred to see them untrammelled
by saddle and bridle, free to run like the wind
without the hand of man.

It was a pleasant day. Jake's parents were
excellent hosts, and Stephanie was glad she'd
packed something suitable to wear, although she
suspected Rebecca had deliberately toned down
her own appearance to match Stephanie's under-
stated elegance.

Stephanie had attended Flemington racecourse
on several previous occasions, but there was an
elusive magic in being there with Jake, and she had
to steel herself to recognise the attention showered
upon her was only make-believe. It would be all

too easy to forget the pretence—worse, to begin to want it to be real. So she smiled a lot, suffered the warm clasp of his hand over hers, and even managed to stand with apparent unconcern when he draped an arm over her shoulders.

She punted on almost every race, and was genuinely ecstatic when she won, philosophical when the horse she'd backed wasn't placed. The first occasion Jake had teasingly offered her a stake for the next, and she refused, politely, but with a firmness that dared him to insist.

They arrived in Kew shortly before six, driven competently by Bart in the opulence of his Rolls. If one had a choice and possessed the wealth to indulge it, a Rolls was the ultimate in motoring experience, Stephanie perceived with a wry little smile. The more she thought about it, the more she was able to understand Alana's desperate bid to hang on. A Rolls-Royce, a penthouse suite in one of Melbourne's prestigious inner city suburbs indicated considerable family wealth. Even Jake's Lamborghini was a rich man's extravagance a preferred few could afford.

'Ah, it will be nice not to have to cook dinner,' Rebecca observed as they rode the elevator to the uppermost floor. 'At Jake's insistence we're dining out.' She sent a smile towards Stephanie. 'Although Bart and I won't party on to a nightclub afterwards. We'll leave that to you younger ones.'

When it came to deciding what to wear, there was only one choice, and Stephanie blessed feminine intuition in having packed the uncrushable synthetic black silk evening trousers and matching blouson top. It was a classic 'go anywhere' outfit, and dressed up with strappy high-heeled sandals, gold chains round her neck, a gold bangle or two on her wrist, it would be eminently suitable.

Only by adopting a blasé approach was she able to sail through showering, changing, alternating use of the bedroom with Jake with the minimum of embarrassment—hers, not his. It was at times like these she wished she'd had a brother. At least now she wouldn't blush at the sight of a male form wearing only a towel hitched carelessly at the waist. From the look of sardonic amusement evident, she suspected he deliberately set out to shock, and it took considerable effort to maintain a calm front.

The restaurant was both intimate and exclusive, the food and wine without fault, and Stephanie began to relax and enjoy herself. With sophisticated adroitness the conversation was never allowed to develop a lull, and after her second glass of wine the evening took on a special illusory glow. It became so easy to smile with genuine warmth when the three people at her table seemed intent on ensuring her enjoyment. For a moment she allowed herself the folly of believing it was all real, and felt incredibly sad. To be loved and cherished, and be able to give in return, must be the ultimate experience. So many tried and had to settle for less, or never settled at all.

'You've become quiet,' Rebecca observed with a kindly smile, and Stephanie forced her eyes to lighten as she summoned a suitable rejoinder.

'It must be the wine,' she dismissed, and her lips parted to form a humorous smile. 'Any more than two glasses and I begin to feel sleepy.'

'A stroll in the fresh air will soon cure that,' Bart asserted, glancing towards his wife. 'Shall we leave?'

'Oh yes, darling, let's,' Rebecca agreed. 'I'm rather tired, and besides, I'm sure Jake would prefer to have Stephanie all to himself.'

Stephanie opened her mouth to demur, then endeavoured not to show her surprise as Jake leaned forward and brushed his lips against the vulnerable pulsing cord at the side of her throat.

'Do you want to go on somewhere else, or shall we stay here?' he murmured, meeting her slightly startled gaze with lazy intimacy. 'They have a small dance floor, and the music is strictly conventional.'

'Are you sure you don't want to go home?' The words were out before she could stop them, and she felt particularly vulnerable as their implication registered.

'Not yet.' His smile was warm and vaguely teasing as he witnessed her confusion, then he glanced towards his parents. 'We'll get a taxi back.'

'Enjoy yourselves,' Rebecca bade gently, and Stephanie could only nod as she watched them vacate their seats.

When they had gone Jake leaned forward and refilled her glass, then his own. 'Here's to us,' he said softly, and Stephanie ignored the faint mockery evident, lifting the glass to her lips as she acknowledged,

'The success of a venture steeped in deceit and duplicity.'

She saw his eyes harden, and his drawled response held a hint of steel. 'I think you've had enough.'

With deliberate movements she slowly drained her glass and replaced it on to the table. 'Really? I've never been drunk in my life, and I certainly don't intend to start now.'

'Let's dance.'

It wasn't a question, merely a command, and she felt vaguely resentful. 'What if I don't want to?'

'You're treading dangerous ground,' Jake murmured with unmistakable menace. 'Continue, and you may not like the consequences.'

'Ah, *punishment*,' she drawled, tilting her head to one side as she regarded him. 'A slap on the hand? I dare you to administer one anywhere else.'

'There are methods more subtle,' he drawled, and suddenly the desire to taunt and bandy words lost impetus.

'I'd like to go home—my home.'

'Not possible.'

'Your parents are nice,' she said slowly. 'Far too nice to deceive. I'm not sure I can keep up the pretence for another day.'

'You will,' Jake declared inflexibly, and standing to his feet he caught hold of her hand and drew her up from her chair. 'We'll dance, have coffee, then have the taxi-driver take us home.'

'Jake——'

'Shut up, there's a good girl, and just melt into my arms like a fiancée should, hmm?'

It was all too easy to obey, although the advisability of doing so was definitely suspect. Being held close against him was both agony and ecstasy, and after a while she didn't want to distinguish between the two. *Now* was all she cared about. Tomorrow would be soon enough for rational reasoning.

At some stage she was aware of being led back to their table, of Jake paying the bill, and the taxi which pulled up to the kerb when they emerged from the main entrance.

Seated in the rear, she leaned back and cushioned her head against Jake's shoulder as if it was the most natural thing in the world to do.

'Are we taking the long way back?'

She could almost sense his wry humour. 'Do you want to?'

'Oh, I think so,' she managed slowly. 'If you're going to kiss me, I'd rather it be now than——'

'Later?' His lips brushed hers, then slid up towards her temple. 'That's debatable.' His instructions to the driver were clear and concise.

As the vehicle eased forward her hands moved of their own volition to clasp together behind his neck, and a warm languorous ache began deep within as his mouth trailed slowly across her cheekbones, closing each eyelid in turn before tracing a path down to the edge of her mouth.

With infinite gentleness he took her lower lip between both of his and outlined its fullness with his tongue, then he probed the softness of her mouth before seeking the deep pulsing cord at her neck. Next came the vulnerable hollows at the base of her throat, and she gave a silent gasp as his head moved lower to the exposed cleft between her breasts.

With a touch so evocative she almost cried out loud, he slid the silky material aside and aroused one hardening bud to an erotic peak before rendering a similar treatment to its twin.

Then slowly his mouth trailed up and closed over hers, possessing with a passionate depth that had her silently groaning with despair. She didn't have the will to resist, nor did she want to as he swept her far out on the tide of ecstasy until she became lost, drowning in a sensual pleasure so tumultuous she never wanted to surface.

Their arrival outside the Kew apartment block was an anti-climax, and she waited in bemused silence as Jake paid the driver, then together they walked hand-in-hand towards the main entrance.

In the elevator she caught a glimpse of herself in the mirrored panel. Wide luminous eyes gazed back, their expression warm and slumbrous. Her mouth bore the swollen evidence of Jake's possession, but it didn't stop there. Her whole body pulsed with a deep aching awareness, a need so great it was a tangible pain.

She couldn't look at him—daren't, for fear of what she might read in his expression, and when they reached the uppermost level she preceded him out into the foyer, waiting silently as he slid a key into the lock.

Rebecca had left a few lights on, but Stephanie didn't falter as she continued through the lounge to their suite. Once there she eased the straps of her heeled sandals and stepped out of them, then moved towards the bed intent on retrieving her pyjamas from beneath the pillow.

'You're not sleeping anywhere but here,' Jake drawled softly from behind, and she stilled, hardly daring to move as his hands settled on her shoulders, then slid down to her waist.

The latent sensuality in his voice was a potent persuasion that made her knees weaken and turn to water, and her heart quickened until its beat seemed to fill her ears with its deafening crescendo. As his lips touched her vulnerable nape she seemed to melt, giving herself totally to the multitude of sensations that coursed through her body like molten fire.

Why not? a tiny voice demanded. At least afterwards she'd have something to remember.

His hands turned her towards him, bringing her close against his hardening frame, and she exulted in his arousal, letting her body mould into his like the twin halves of a whole.

The mouth that closed over hers held a fierce passion, its possession hungry and demanding, rendering her almost mindless as he began to divest her of her clothes with practised ease.

It was only when he had removed most of his own that warning bells began clamouring inside her brain, and when he lifted her into his arms and swung her down on to the large bed she went suddenly still.

'Stephanie?' His voice was thick with desire, and while part of her triumphed, she was filled with an inescapable fear that at this precise moment any woman would meet his needs.

'I—can't.' The words came out as a tortured whisper, and her eyes welled, then overflowed. Realisation of how close she had come made her tremble, and her hands shook as she pushed ineffectually against his shoulders. 'Please—let me go.'

Jake's husky oath was a frightening reminder of the tenuous rein of his control, and she froze, appalled that any movement might precipitate an assault she would be powerless to prevent.

'I'm supposed to switch off,' Jake muttered roughly. 'Just like that?'

His body was tense with suppressed violence, and it seemed as if time became a suspended entity as she waited, hardly daring to breathe for fear of unleashing any or all of that pent-up emotion.

'Do you realise I could take you *now*?' he demanded savagely, and his hands closed cruelly over her shoulders until she gasped with the pain.

'Damn you, Stephanie—damn you to hell!' he muttered softly, rolling on to his back to lie beside her, and she began to shake as reaction began to take its effect.

'I'm sorry,' she whispered hesitantly, endless minutes later.

'Dear God—at least spare me any platitudes!'

The seconds ticked slowly by, and she offered achingly, 'I won't be a substitute.'

'Careful, my sweet,' he drawled silkily. 'This is hardly the appropriate time for sanctimonious revelations. If you've an ounce of sense, you'll lie very still and not utter a further word.'

He had no need to elaborate, and in the darkness the tears welled and spilled to run slowly down her cheeks, soaking the pillow.

CHAPTER NINE

WHEN Stephanie woke next morning there was only an indentation in the pillow next to hers to provide a palpable reminder of their tortuous conflict. Of Jake there was no sign, and she cautiously slid from the bed, catching up her robe to cover her nakedness before crossing to the bathroom.

A quick shower restored a measure of warmth, and towelled dry, she completed her toilette, pulled on fresh underwear and donned tailored slacks and a patterned knit jumper. Make-up was minimal, just a thin film of moisturiser followed by a touch of colour to her lips, and she brushed her hair with unwarranted vigour until the natural curls sprang back in protest.

It was after eight; and there seemed no sense in delaying the inevitable confrontation with Jake. At least Rebecca and Bart would provide an essential buffer. The crunch, if any, would come later when they were alone.

The lounge was deserted, and she crossed to the dining-room, summoning a bright smile the instant before she entered. Bart was seated at the table, newspaper in hand, and there were sounds of occupation accompanied by a tantalising aroma from the direction of the kitchen.

'Good morning, my dear,' he greeted her warmly, his eyes creasing with kindled affection as she returned his welcome. 'Rebecca is fixing breakfast. I doubt she needs any assistance, but go through anyway.'

'Hmm,' she responded lightly. 'It makes me feel hungry.' The effort of keeping up a suitable appearance would probably kill her by the end of the day, she perceived mentally.

'If my wife won't have you in the kitchen, come and join me for coffee.'

'Shall do,' Stephanie promised.

Rebecca glanced up from stirring eggs in a frypan, and her smiled echoed her husband's warmth. 'Hi there. Jake should be back soon. He left early for a work-out in the gym.' Glimpsing Stephanie's unbidden surprise, she elaborated, 'The entire first floor is given over to recreational facilities. Next time you come, you must use them.'

Except there won't be a next time, Stephanie thought hollowly, and wondered why she felt so bereft. She managed a suitable rejoinder and offered to set the table.

She had just completed the chore when Jake walked into the room, and there was nothing she could do to prevent her stomach performing a series of somersaults before it tightened into a painful ball. She watched in mesmerised fascination as he crossed to her side, and she was sure he could hear her heart thud as he trailed an idle finger across her lips.

He didn't say a word, and she proffered a tremulous smile, unsure of what he intended. To an onlooker he bore the appearance of casual ruggedness, the pale grey of his tracksuit accentuating a powerful frame, and only Stephanie glimpsed the faint brooding darkness in his eyes before it was masked.

Breakfast was a leisurely meal, and afterwards, attired in warm outdoor clothes, they set off for Cowes on the southern peninsula of Phillip Island.

'We adore getting away from the city at weekends,' Rebecca explained as the Rolls sped smoothly down the highway. 'Bart is an accomplished barbecue chef, and unless the weather is too miserable we usually stop at a picnic ground for lunch. When Melinda and Evan are home, there's the children as well.'

'Melinda is my dutiful sister,' Jake drawled in explanation, and on glimpsing his mother's surprise he added sardonically,

'Stephanie and I have had other things on our mind.'

Her faint blush didn't go unnoticed, but its cause wasn't as Rebecca imagined. Nonetheless she was amused by the chiding chastisement heaped on Jake's head, and she appeared suitably grateful to learn more details about the Stanton family.

The weather provided weak winter sunshine, bracing fresh air, and at a picnic spot close to the ocean there was a tang of salt that did wonders for the appetite. Thanks to Jake's parents' efforts the day was a success, although the strain of continually wearing a smile began to have an effect, and as the hours flew by Stephanie became increasingly aware of their approaching departure.

'You're looking rather pale,' Rebecca observed anxiously from the front seat. 'I do hope we haven't let you overdo things.'

Stephanie demurred at once, and had to contain her surprise as Jake caught hold of her chin and tilted it towards him.

'Hmm,' he drawled, subjecting her to a raking scrutiny. 'I think we'll head back.' His expression was an inscrutable mask, and she kept her lashes lowered so he couldn't read their depths.

'You will stay for dinner?' Rebecca queried, brushing aside his dissent. 'It will be much more sensible to eat with us, then Stephanie is spared having to prepare food when you get home.'

That seemed to take care of that, Stephanie decided wryly, glad of a slight reprieve as Jake conceded his mother's logic.

In the Kew penthouse she was careful not to be alone with him, and succeeded until just prior to dinner when it became imperative to pack the few clothes she had brought.

The chore didn't take long, and she closed the zip fastening and placed the bag on the floor near the door.

'You resemble a scared little rabbit, poised for imminent flight,' Jake drawled with hateful cynicism. His glance was cool and totally devoid of any emotion. 'You're quite safe here, Stephanie,' he added with soft emphasis. 'And it really won't do for you to scurry away so quickly. After all,' he taunted, 'we're supposed to be wrapped up in each other to the extent we can hardly bear to be apart.' His eyes fell to her mouth, then slid slowly up to spear her gaze. 'Those sweet lips should look kissed, don't you think?'

Her eyes widened with a mixture of hurt reproach and silent pleading as he moved slowly towards her. Without her being aware of it her hands moved to form a gesture of entreaty. 'Please, don't!'

He was within touching distance, and she sank back against the wall, flattening herself in an attempt to elude him.

With seeming effortlessness he reached for her, pulling her close until she was made hauntingly aware of his hard length, then one hand slid to enfold her even closer while the other moved to hold fast her head.

As his mouth lowered she made one last desperate bid to escape, then her lips were taken, possessed and plundered in a kiss that was punishingly cruel.

There was no passion evident—certainly no pleasure, and when he finally released her she could only stand swaying, her body numbed into immobility by his deliberate onslaught.

'Don't look at me like that!' Jake ground out emotively, and she made a gesture of impunity, unable to voice so much as a single word.

Slowly she turned, intent on getting away from him. In the bathroom she ran water into the basin and sluiced her face, first with hot water, then with cold. She wanted to cry, but such a childish indulgence was a luxury she couldn't afford. Slowly she towelled her face dry, then glanced up to see Jake leaning against the door-jamb watching her.

She had packed her make-up, and she moved past him to retrieve it from her overnight bag. In a way it would serve him right if she didn't attempt to repair the ravages he'd wrought, and only the thought of upsetting Rebecca ensured that she took great care with her appearance.

Dinner was one of the most difficult meals she had ever sat through, and as if sensing her distress Jake displayed marked tenderness, explaining that she was suffering a headache—ironic, when he was the direct cause of it, she decided darkly as she tried to field his parents' concern.

Afterwards it was relatively easy to thank them both for an enjoyable weekend. Their hospitality had been without fault, their genuine efforts to make her welcome held a bittersweet poignancy, and there was real regret as Stephanie bade them goodbye.

Ensconced in the Lamborghini, she simply leaned back, closed her eyes, and let the classical tape Jake inserted wash over her as he drove swiftly and silently along the Western highway.

When the car drew to a halt in the wide sweeping driveway she slid out, walked the few steps to the front entrance, inserted her key, then ascended the stairs to her room.

It was barely nine, but she felt too enervated to do anything but undress and slip wearily into bed.

On the edge of sleep she heard the soft click of her door being opened, followed by the almost inaudible pad of animal tread accompanied by a slight whimper as Satan sank down on to the floor, then she heard Jake's retreating footfalls as he moved down the hall.

It was then that the tears fell, and with acute perception the German Shepherd lifted his head and rested it on the edge of her pillow, the only witness to his mistress's desolation.

News of their engagement had become an established fact, and continuing to field the numerable phone calls from friends, wellwishers and the overtly curious became increasingly difficult.

Stephanie threw herself boundlessly into a seemingly endless number of chores, ensuring with frenetic energy that she didn't have a minute to spare. Avoiding Jake became an exercise in which she excelled, and by Friday she was counting the hours until her father's return.

If Jake noticed, he made no comment, although more than once he appeared on the verge of unloosing a pithy diatribe, and Jim Matheson's keen observation of her wan state brought a dark speaking glance that made her glad of her father's presence.

As to her engagement, her father's delight merely served to compound the mockery, and it seemed unbearably cruel that he should be so deliberately misled.

Fortunately both men retired to the study immediately after dinner in an effort to catch up on everything that had transpired over the past month, and Stephanie was glad she was spared the effort of having to maintain an affectionate, even loving, façade. At nine she took them coffee, pleaded a headache and retired to bed.

Sunday dawned with overcast skies and the promise of rain. By midday the house was being lashed with wind-whipped squalls, and Stephanie mused darkly that the weather was an adequate reflection of her mood.

Jake's departure was loosely timed for late afternoon, and as it drew near she could only regard his impending absence with a sense of relief. The tension between them had built up to a dangerous level, putting her on edge to a degree whereby she felt as if she was walking a proverbial tightrope.

'I'll let you see Jake to the door,' Jim Matheson smiled, and the corners of his eyes crinkled with gentle humour. 'I'm sure you want a few minutes alone.'

If only you knew! Stephanie thought wildly, momentarily torn between refusal and compliance. Jake settled it by taking hold of her hand, and loath to create a scene, she had little choice but to follow him from the room.

'Don't you dare touch me!' she hissed vehemently as they reached the foyer, and she almost cringed from the icy anger evident in his dark eyes.

'Oh, come, darling,' he drawled, pulling her close. 'A fiancé has a right to a farewell kiss, surely?'

'Couldn't we dispense with it?' she queried hollowly, silently willing him to relent. 'There's no one around to see.'

His mouth curved down to form a cynical smile. 'I shan't ravish you, if that's what you're afraid of.'

Won't you? she queried silently, hating the way her body seemed to be reaching out of its own accord towards him.

Even as his head descended she steeled herself against an unenviable onslaught, expecting him to wreak revenge. Instead, his mouth closed over hers in an evocative possession, warm and insistently probing as he explored its softness. It held a leashed passion, and something more—regret?

Even as he drew away she dismissed the feeling as being fanciful. He was probably just as pleased to leave as she was to see him go. Yet an inner voice rose unbidden in silent derision to taunt her, and she stood perfectly still as he trailed an idle finger down the length of her tiptilted nose.

'I'll phone within a few days, okay?'

'Sure,' she responded tremulously, and her eyes filled with ignominious tears as he opened the door and moved quickly down to the car.

He didn't look back, and she was filled with an incredible desolation as she watched the red glow of the Lamborghini's tail-lights disappear down the driveway.

If her bleakness was noticed it was no doubt

construed to be a normal reaction, and although she strove valiantly to present a reasonably bright front, her attempts for the most part were a dismal failure.

When the phone rang Wednesday evening she lifted the receiver with mounting trepidation, and her heart gave a painful lurch at the sound of Jake's voice.

'Missing me?'

His soft taunting cynicism acted like a dash of cold water, and she responded with unaccustomed flippancy. 'Am I meant to?'

'Obviously you're alone,' he mused sardonically.

'Obviously.' It was true, for her father had been called to the clinic to conduct emergency surgery on an accident case.

'I have news,' Jake relayed without preamble. 'The private detective I employed to report Alana's movements has reported that she flew out of the country this morning.'

A pain like a fist closing round her heart was so intense she almost cried out with it. 'Then it's all over,' she said quietly.

'I promised you a holiday. Let me know when you can organise a week off so that I can make suitable arrangements.'

'No.' The single word emerged from her throat in a strangled whisper.

'For the love of heaven——'

'I don't want anything from you, Jake.'

She could sense his anger, and felt strangely detached.

'Dammit, Stephanie——'

'Goodbye,' she managed evenly, then replaced the receiver before she burst into tears.

CHAPTER TEN

THE days numbered slowly up to form a week—
days in which she could neither eat nor sleep, and
soon was seen to visibly lose weight, her finely
moulded features becoming more sharply etched
until both her father and Mrs Anderson took her
to task.

The brilliant diamond she had reluctantly worn
only served as a mocking reminder, and with
renewed resolve she slid it off, parcelled it up,
insured and despatched it to Jake at his parents'
address.

A week went by, followed by another, the
pattern of each day a desultory imitation of its
predecessor. She persistently refused to lead a
social existence, and retired into a protective shell
that neither Karen nor even Michael could
penetrate.

The adage about time being a great healer might
hold some truth, but after a month Stephanie
viewed its logic with some scepticism. Her appetite
had improved slightly, but only as an attempt to
allay her father's concern. The nights were
something else. No matter how she tried she
couldn't dismiss Jake's forceful image. It continually rose to taunt her, disturbing her sleep and
providing a palpable reminder.

Nothing dulled the pain, and even Michael's
goodnatured humour did little to lift her flagging
spirits. Only the animals provided some solace,
and she became so involved in caring for the sick

and the stray that even her father insisted she deploy her interest, at least in part, elsewhere.

Stephanie tried, without success. Taking in a movie with Karen, even attending a party with Michael didn't help, despite their efforts to make each outing enjoyable. What was the use when her gaze unconsciously searched every tall dark-haired male head for a glimpse of a man she knew she would never see again?

Jim Matheson's suggestion that she take a week or more and holiday in the warm Queensland sunshine evoked an outright refusal, until being confronted with an airline ticket and hotel reservation left her little choice but to accept.

Hayman Island, at the head of the Whitsunday group in North Queensland, was an idyllic tropical paradise noted for its translucent waters, an abundance of varied tropical reef fish, and above all, a calm relaxing atmosphere.

For a week Stephanie did nothing but laze beneath the sun, read, swim, and attempt to get her life into some sort of perspective. Certainly she gained a great tan, and her appetite improved measurably, but as a strategy to banish Jake from her mind it was a dismal failure.

Jim Matheson was at the airport on her return, and she glimpsed his kindly face among the waiting crowd an instant before he saw her, and she summoned a dazzling smile as she moved forward to greet him.

'Let me look at you.' He drew back and regarded her intently. 'Not my dear sweet Stephanie, but definitely an improvement on the girl who left here last week.'

'I'm fine—really,' she assured him lightly. 'Did you get my postcards?'

'Yes, as did Michael, and Karen.' His blue eyes speared hers with kindly affection. 'Didn't you do anything else but write cryptic little messages to us all?'

'Of course. Haven't you noticed my tan?' she teased. 'I read two hefty novels currently high on the bestseller list, flipped through at least a dozen magazines, and watched all the soap operas on television. Satisfied?'

'Not entirely,' he responded honestly. 'But you'll do.'

She made a miniature curtsy. 'Thank you, kind sir. Now, if we're all through with the "hello-how-are-you" bit, we'd better collect my luggage.'

At home Satan gave her an enthusiastic welcome, as did all the other animals, and she fondled the German Shepherd's ears with affection. 'Man's best friend, aren't you?'

'They've all missed you,' her father said quietly. 'So have I.'

Stephanie crossed and gave him a warm hug, then kissed his leathery cheek. 'I've missed you, too,' she assured him softly. 'You're a very dear man, whom I happen to love very much.'

His eyes seemed to acquire a glimmer for a few seconds, then he grinned. 'I suppose you're going to insist on coming into the clinic tomorrow?'

'Of course.'

And she did, with an equanimity that had Michael softly whistling with approval.

The following few days were busy as she caught up with the monthly accounts and various other secretarial chores the temporary girl hadn't managed to achieve. The state of the files indicated a lack of sufficient care, and it took considerable time to get them all into a semblance of order.

On Thursday Stephanie drove into town, and after mailing the accounts and completing the banking she slipped into a near-by café and ordered a sandwich and coffee.

It was almost two o'clock when she eased her Datsun out of its parking space and sent it into the main stream of traffic. The day was remarkably clear; one of those rare early spring days when the sun's warmth gave a prelude of what was to come. Most of the trees were still bare, but the countryside had lost the heavy green mantle of winter and the earth seemed to hold a waiting expectancy for the emergence of a new season's growth.

Stephanie eased the sports coupé into the driveway, and sent it speeding towards the house. Her actions were guided by experience and the sheer familiarity of having traversed the gravelled driveway countless times before.

There were a few cars lining the curved apron of asphalt adjacent to the clinic, and declining to enter the garage she turned the car towards the stand of trees bordering the side of the house.

A patch of gleaming silver metal entered her peripheral vision, and the breath caught in her throat as she recognised the sleek low lines of Jake's Lamborghini.

Oh God! There were any number of reasons for his presence at the clinic, yet at this precise moment she could think of only one. *Fool*, she accorded with self-derisive bitterness. He'd walked away, out of her life, without so much as a backward glance. He wasn't likely to walk back in.

A hysterical bubble of laughter rose in her throat as she moved her foot to the accelerator. There was no power on earth strong enough to give her sufficient courage to enter the clinic and deal with the effect his presence would have.

Uncaring that her actions might be noticed and commented upon, she sent the car back down the driveway, and once clear of the cattle-grid she headed in the opposite direction of town.

Why—*why*? she groaned inaudibly. Just when she'd thought she could handle his absence, he had to return, bringing alive a wealth of memories far too vivid ever to be consigned into oblivion.

Unbidden, his image rose to taunt her. Eyes as deep and unfathomable as an ocean, and remote; warm and liquid with silent laughter; slumbrous with passion. She knew their every expression, and had become more aware of her own sexuality within his arms that she had ever dreamed possible. And his mouth—even to imagine its curving lines, the sensual promise and the torment its touch could wreak plunged her into a state of such despair she could hardly *see*.

Whether by instinct or pure reflex action, she cast a glance at her rear-vision mirror, and almost died as she recognised the car travelling close behind.

Her breathing became ragged and painful, her heartbeat reaching an impossible thunderous crescendo as she glimpsed the Lamborghini's racy body swing out and draw alongside.

She risked a sideways glance, trying to gauge his intention, and saw him motion for her to pull over.

Damn his arrogant hide! If he thought she'd meekly follow his direction, he had another think coming!

Foot almost to the floor, she sent the car surging forward, indifferent at that moment of any risk to life and limb. Seventy, eighty, ninety, the speedometer needle swung steadily higher. All her nerve-ends screamed in agonising rejection, bringing a return to sanity, and even as she began to brake there was a flash of silver metal as the Lamborghini streaked past, its throttled back speed forcing her to come to a slow halt at the edge of the road.

The engine was still running, and she automatically reached out to switch off the ignition. The resultant silence became a suspended entity, and with an inaudible groan she let her head fall down on to the steering wheel in a gesture of utter defeat.

Through a mist of despair she heard the decisive clunk of a car door closing, followed by the crunch of footsteps on the road's gravelled edge, then her door was wrenched open and firm hands reached in and released her seatbelt.

'You crazy idiotic little *fool*!' His voice was full of barely controlled fury. 'Get out!'

How dared he issue orders? A slow burning rage rose to the surface, and she leaned back against the seat, her eyes alive with anger as she swung round to face him. 'The *hell* I will!'

Dark brown eyes glinted with icy resolve. 'Then move over, and I'll get in.'

'No!' The single denial left her lips as an agonised groan. It was bad enough him being here. At least she felt some measure of protection seated within the car.

'It's one or the other, Stephanie,' Jake growled emotively. 'You want me to decide?'

He looked angry enough to do her bodily harm, and she felt oddly threatened. 'What is this?' she managed icily. 'Another example of imposed harassment?'

A muscle tensed along his jaw, and his gaze narrowed fractionally. 'You want revenge?'

Her eyes became fiery blue chips, brilliant and fiercely angry. '*Yes*—damn you!'

'Then get out and take it.'

For a moment she was tempted, then reason returned. 'Oh?' she inclined with intended sarcasm. 'Should I beat my fists against your chest, kick your shins—physically *slap* you?' A slightly hysterical laugh escaped her lips. 'I'm not crazy enough to imagine you'd let me!'

His voice was a silky drawl and infinitely dangerous. 'It could only have one ending.'

Stephanie momentarily closed her eyes against the picture his words evoked, and he stated quietly—

'The ultimate revenge would be to let me walk to my car and drive out of your life.'

She was still consumed with rage and bitterness, and the desire to hurt was uppermost. 'Then walk, Jake. *Walk!*'

The silence was electrifying, then he said slowly, 'If you're sure that's what you want.'

Why did his voice sound so stiff—even *bleak*? Almost as if he cared. Yet he couldn't—could he?

Stephanie heard his footsteps begin to recede, one by one, and she watched his tall frame with mesmerised fascination. With a sense of dawning horror her mind leapt ahead, mentally envisaging the damnable hell of having to watch him leave.

The thought of never seeing him again, the need to know *why* he'd come back, the full importance of his words, clamoured for supremacy, and with startling clarity she knew that revenge and pride had no place in her emotions.

'Jake.' In her haste to get out of the car she

almost tripped, and her hand clutched at the door for support, then she broke into a run. *'Jake!'*

He paused, but didn't turn, and she faltered to a halt at his side.

'I was angry,' she offered quietly.

'Are you still?'

'I thought I had a right to be.'

A muscle tensed along his jaw, the only movement visible in that grim profile. 'And now?'

Stephanie swallowed the sudden lump that had risen in her throat. 'I think you'd better tell me why you came back,' she began slowly. 'Especially why you followed me out here.'

His lips took on a cynical twist. 'Your pound of flesh, Stephanie?'

Sudden pain clouded her vision, and her voice ached with agonising emotion. 'Aren't I entitled to some explanation?'

It seemed a long time before he answered, and when he did his voice was curiously detached.

'Alana had become a problem. She had my parents' address and her calls were a nuisance—to them, and to me. Your father's offer couldn't have come at a more appropriate time. What I hadn't bargained for was you,' he conferred with a self-mocking grimace. 'I wanted to ignore you, except in a professional capacity during clinic hours. However, fate took a hand, and Mrs James' untimely accident threw us into constant contact— with some disastrous results. You aroused unenviable emotions, not the least of which was a strong desire to get you into my bed. I told myself it had to be a basic greed of the flesh, but I was wrong. It went much deeper than that.' He lifted a hand as if to touch her, then let it fall back to his side.

'When I left, I thought I could walk away and

forget everything that had happened. God knows I tried. I became a sought-after escort to a bevy of beautiful young things who could have been mine if I'd shown the merest inclination, but the only face I could see was yours. Your smile, eyes as blue as an ocean and deep enough for a man to drown in. I cursed you a thousand times for giving me a glimpse of heaven—something I'd assured myself I was better off without.' His hand moved abstractedly to his hair, raking through its well-groomed length and ruffling it into attractive disorder.

'I lifted the phone to call you, only to slam down the receiver before I'd dialled the full requisite of digits. I became a positive bear,' he revealed with rueful cynicism. 'Unreasonable to work with, and equally impossible at home. Eventually I reached the point where I had to see you again—the warm flesh and blood *you*, not the image I carried constantly in my head. That was when I rang—twice,' he added with a mocking smile. 'Only to be met with an uncategorical refusal to even speak to me. Up until then I hadn't given our possible future much thought. There was no doubt I wanted you, but after one disastrous marriage I wasn't keen to embark on another.'

Stephanie hardly dared breathe. It seemed as if her whole life hung in the balance, and her heartbeat began to quicken, like a trapped bird apprehensive of its plight.

'I want you with me,' he said quietly, adding with deliberate emphasis, 'Every day, all through the night. For the rest of my life.'

Every single body hair tingled alive, and each delicate sensory nerve-end began to pulse with an increased longing until she felt as if she was on fire. 'Are you sure?'

His eyes were dark with passionate intensity, and pain. 'Walk into my arms, and I'll show you exactly how sure.'

A sudden prick of tears misted her vision. 'I love you,' she whispered tremulously.

Strong arms reached out and enfolded her close against him, holding her as if they would never let her go, then his mouth was on hers, hungry and infinitely passionate as he sought to wipe out all the bitterness and uncertainty.

It was a long time before he released her, and she buried her head against his chest, overwhelmed by the strength of his emotion, and her own. There was so much she wanted to say, and she would, given time. But some things couldn't wait.

Slowly she lifted her head, her eyes startlingly direct as she met and held his with clarity. 'I didn't think love could hurt so much. It frightened me, wondering if the attraction—the mystical physical emotion we shared was anything more than desire. For you.' She paused, struggling to find the right words. 'I went through the tortures of the damned, unwilling to face the implications Alana had in your life. I couldn't forget that I was convenient in your scheme of things, and much as I wanted to believe otherwise, there didn't seem any point in adding to my heartache. Why should you be attracted to a girl like me?' she queried simply. 'A man who could take his pick of any nubile blonde, brunette or redhead, for that matter. That was when the bitterness began, and the anger.' An inherent honesty made her qualify, 'Mostly against myself for not being realistic.'

'Fool,' Jake muttered softly, trailing his lips down to tease the edge of her mouth. 'Mmm, I could easily become addicted to this.' He savoured the sweetness of her lips, then traced an evocative path down to the hollow at the base of her throat.

'Could you?'

'Oh yes,' he acknowledged gently. 'Can't you feel it?'

A soft pink tinged her cheeks and he laughed at her confusion, pulling her even closer against him so that she could be in no doubt of his arousal.

'We're standing on the road in the midst of a public thoroughfare,' she murmured with a shaky laugh, and a passing car gave a loud hornblast as if to emphasise her words.

'Let's go somewhere private.' His slow smile melted her bones, and her lips formed a slight protest.

'It's the middle of the afternoon.'

'What has that got to do with anything?' Jake mused with faint irony, and some of her tremulous uncertainty communicated itself. '*Stephanie*,' he chided, giving her a slight shake, 'I love you. Oh hell, I haven't even told you, have I?' His hands slid up to cup her face, his expression infinitely gentle. 'Two days from now, we'll be married. I have the licence, and your father's sanction.'

It didn't sink in at first, and when it did, she could only look at him with a sense of wonderment. 'You're not serious?'

'You crazy little idiot,' he grated roughly. 'Do you honestly think I could live with you, *love* you, and not make it legal?' His mouth closed over hers with punishing bruising force until she gasped for breath.

'I can't believe it!'

A slow smile teased his lips, and his eyes gleamed with sudden laughter. 'I shall have to make it my business to see that you do.'

A devilish grin widened her generous mouth, lightening her eyes until they sparkled like fiery blue sapphires. 'Really?'

'Did I tell you how beautiful you are?' Jake queried gently. 'I could never tire of just looking at you. Skin as soft as silk to the touch, hair that smells like crushed wildflowers.' His mouth sought a vulnerable hollow in a provocative caress. 'I love you.' There was serious intent in his voice, almost a dedication. 'I'm taking you home, where, after a suitable time, I shall bid you goodnight and book into a motel.'

She was unable to stop the incredulous query, 'Why? You could easily stay at the house.'

'I daren't,' he admitted ruefully, shooting her a wry smile. 'And you shouldn't have to ask why.'

'Jake Stanton—bowing down to convention?' A tiny laugh bubbled up inside her. 'I don't believe it!'

His kiss was punishingly brief. 'Believe, Stephanie. When I share your bed, I want my ring on your finger, and the whole night in which to love you. What's more, I want to wake up with you beside me. "With this body, I thee worship",' he quoted softly. 'And I intend to, for the rest of my life.'

Her lips quivered, and there were tears shimmering her eyes as she was torn between the desire to laugh and cry. 'Oh, Jake!'

His eyes darkened with smouldering warmth, then his mouth twisted into a wry smile. 'Let's go,' he slanted roughly, leaning forward to open her car door, and after pushing her gently into the driver's seat, he bent down and issued the soft command, 'Follow me.'

Stephanie felt her lips curve into a winsome

smile, and her eyes were alive with the intensity of her emotions.

For a moment he hesitated, and she revelled in the depth of passion evident in his expressive gaze, then he smiled and turned towards the Lamborghini.

Seconds later the powerful engine fired, and she watched as it slowly turned round and headed back along the highway. She sent the Datsun in its wake, travelling at a sedate speed until, one behind the other, they traversed the long curving driveway leading up to the clinic.

Stephanie brought the sports coupé to a halt outside the garage, then she slid out and took hold of Jake's outstretched hand, and together they walked slowly towards the house.

They were married on Saturday afternoon, a short civil ceremony with only both immediate families present.

Stephanie wore a dress of cream silk and carried an exquisite spray of orchids, while Jake was resplendent in a dark three-piece suit and immaculate white linen.

Their vows were exchanged with quiet solemnity, and afterwards there was a buffet dinner prepared by Mrs Anderson at the house.

Rebecca and Bart, Jake's sister Melinda, her husband Evan and their two children were present, and Stephanie was delighted to see Michael and Karen, together with a few close family friends.

There were champagne toasts conveying good wishes, and it was after nine when Stephanie and Jake managed to slip away. Their honeymoon destination was Hawaii, but tonight they were driving to Melbourne and staying in a motel.

Stephanie preceded Jake inside the luxurious apartment and moved towards the lounge.

'I believe there's champagne on ice,' he murmured, turning towards her. 'Shall I open a bottle?'

'If you like.' She tried to appear calm, but tranquillity wasn't uppermost in her thoughts right now. Nervousness had to be responsible for the way her tongue edged out over her lower lip, and her eyes felt incredibly large as she watched him move slowly towards her.

When he was within touching distance he reached out and trailed his fingers gently down her cheek. 'On the other hand, we could dispense with the champagne and go straight to bed.' A slight smile deepened the sensual curve of his mouth as he glimpsed the faint blush tinging her cheeks. 'Come here,' he commanded softly, and reaching out he pulled her gently into his arms. 'I need you.' His lips began a slow exploration of her face, finally coming to rest at the edge of her mouth. 'Kiss me, Stephanie.'

She began to tremble, and her voice came out as a strangled whisper. 'I love you.' Her whole body vibrated with the need to be close to him, have him lose himself inside her. It was like an inescapable hunger. Slowly she reached up and clasped her hands behind his neck, pulling his face close, then she hesitantly sought the edge of his mouth. 'I *ache* so much, it's almost indecent,' she said shakily.

'Hmm,' Jake mused teasingly. 'That's a very provocative statement. Perhaps I should do something about it.'

'Starting—when?'

'Oh—I'd say round about now,' he drawled, his hands moulding her slim curves to the taut muscular lines of his body.

'Mmm,' she murmured, giving him a singularly sweet smile. 'Are we through talking?'

'Witch,' he declared huskily as he trailed his lips with a delicate erotic tracery over the planes of her face before slipping to seek a vulnerable hollow at the base of her throat.

A tiny moan left her lips. 'Love me, Jake. *Please*!' Tears filled her eyes and spilled over to run slowly down her cheeks. To be with him like this, to know that they would always be together, filled her with such profound elation it was almost more than she could bear.

His tongue tasted the saltiness of her tears, and he followed their path with such infinite gentleness it only served to increase the flow. 'Why are you crying?' His breath was warm against her cheeks, and she turned her head slightly, unconsciously seeking the possession of his mouth.

Stephanie felt his lips curve into a smile beneath her own, and although his touch was deliberately evocative he didn't deepen the kiss, choosing instead to follow the fullness of her lower lip.

He let his mouth trail slowly down to her chin, then travel lingeringly down her throat to hover teasingly at the soft hollows there before slipping to the curve of her breast which had somehow become exposed to his touch.

There was no part of her body she wouldn't allow him licence to, and her clothes, *his*, were a restricting barrier that were easily dispensed with. Her fingers moved shakily over the fastenings, exulting in the feel of her flesh against the hard muscle and sinew of his.

With a deep husky chuckle Jake led her towards the bed, and she gasped as he pulled her down with him, laughing as his hands grasped her waist

and eased her body forward. Then she groaned as
his mouth closed over the tender peak of her
breast, his tongue circling and teasing the
burgeoning bud until waves of erotic sensation
transcended to the very core of her being. Not
content, he rendered a similar treatment to its
twin, ignoring her pleas, the almost guttural moan
her voice had become as she implored for his
ultimate possession to release the agonising wealth
of sensual fire he had succeeded in arousing.

There wasn't an inch of her body he didn't
explore, and she was totally mindless when at last
he gave her the release she craved.

Afterwards she lay curved protectively against
his body, her head pillowed above his heart. His
arms held her, and his breath fanned the hair at
her temple. Words didn't seem necessary, and
would have been a superfluous intrusion in the
warm wondrous aftermath.

At last, alerted by the shadows of oncoming
dawn, Stephanie lifted a hand and idly traced her
fingers through the mat of chest hairs, creating an
unintentional evocative pattern. 'Are you hungry?'

She could almost sense his smile. 'Should I be?'

A playful tug of her fingers brought forth a
husky growl. 'Food, you insatiable fiend,' she
admonished with a grin, and heard his answering
laugh.

'Ravenous,' Jake told her softly, his eyes
kindling with a slumbrous warmth as she turned
her head up to his, and her heartbeat tripped and
began to thud.

Never would she get used to the tumult he could
cause to her emotions, and she looked at him in
silence, drinking in the look of him, the feel and
smell that was essentially his alone.

'I'll make an early breakfast,' she ventured. 'We have to be at the airport before nine.'

'That gives me an hour,' Jake declared lazily, and as her eyes widened in silent query he slanted a slow teasing smile. 'To love you again,' he elaborated softly, and he proceeded to do so with such infinite gentleness she thought she might drown in an exquisite vortex of emotion.

Afterwards they rose from the bed, then, showered and dressed, they rode a taxi to the airport to board the giant Boeing with minutes to spare.

Stephanie leaned back in her seat and watched the ground disappear below.

'Do you realise how long this flight is?'

A light bubbly laugh rose to the surface, and she turned towards him with a teasing smile. 'Hawaii was your idea.'

'So it was,' Jake declared a trifle wryly. 'I shall see that you bestow suitable compensation.'

She wrinkled her nose at him. 'Behave,' she admonished, her eyes sparkling with humour. 'We're about to be served breakfast. A meal we both missed, if you remember?'

'Remind me to beat you,' he drawled, and she gave an irrepressible grin.

'Is that a threat, or a promise?'

He slanted a look that left her in no doubt of his answer, then he reached out a hand and trailed his fingers down her cheek. 'Happy?'

'Yes,' she answered simply, and almost died at the wealth of latent passion in his gaze.

Ignoring any interested onlookers, he took hold of her hand and lifted it to his lips, then vowed gently, 'I intend making sure you stay that way for the rest of your life.'

Coming Next Month in Harlequin Presents!

751 DARK TYRANT   Helen Bianchin
A young Australian discovers that her stepfather used her as collateral for a loan. Now he's dead. Payment is due—in full. And she's supposed to be thankful that her blackmailer intends to marry her.

752 LETTER FROM BRONZE MOUNTAIN   Rosemary Carter
Love at first sight betrays a South African artist when the man she meets and loses her heart to turns out to be the man she holds responsible for her sister's death.

753 AN INDEPENDENT WOMAN   Claire Harrison
In the clear light of the Canadian Rockies, a sensitive woman is challenged by a forceful man to go with him to the prairies...to find out who she really is.

754 INTIMATE   Donna Huxley
Things go from bad to worse when an unscrupulous executive hounds a young computer researcher out of the firm and out of the job market. But surely the man in her life won't believe the lies!

755 RULES OF THE GAME   Penny Jordan
Beginner's luck doesn't hold up for an English photographer posing as her flamboyantly beautiful cousin when she's disqualified for cheating by the man who wrote the rules for the game of love.

756 THE OPEN MARRIAGE   Flora Kidd
An English furniture designer still loves her Welsh husband, even though she left him once she learned about the other woman in his life. But before she initiates divorce proceedings....

757 UNTAMED   Carole Mortimer
A young, publicity-shy woman attracts the unwanted attentions of an actor who gives a brilliant portrayal of a man in love. If only she could believe him.

758 TOO FAR, TOO FAST   Elizabeth Oldfield
They meet again in Hong Kong and seem fated to sacrifice love a second time for the sake of his professional tennis career. Then they discover the manipulations of a real pro.